Totally Bound Publishing books by Tina Donahue

Taming the Beast
Freeing the Beast
Surrendering to the Beast
Mastering the Beast
Muzzling the Beast
Disciplining the Beast
Seducing the Beast

I0571292

Taming the Beast

SEDUCING THE BEAST

TINA DONAHUE

Seducing the Beast
ISBN # 978-1-83943-831-8
©Copyright Tina Donahue 2019
Cover Art by Posh Gosh ©Copyright February 2019
Interior text design by Claire Siemaszkiewicz
Totally Bound Publishing

SEDUCING THE BEAST

Dedication

To sexy bad boys and the women who capture
their hearts.

Chapter One

Ursula sagged in her chair, hand over her eyes. For three weeks she'd gone through treatment at From Crud to Stud, a New Orleans makeover service for supernatural beings. Instead of these sessions turning her into a bad girl who drew hot men to her, she was still the same blah, frumpy good angel she'd been since ancient times. Talk about her decency getting old and the shameless indulgence she craved not happening as easily as she'd hoped.

She seemed doomed to spend her life alone and unwanted. Her mouth trembled. "This isn't working. It's never going to, for me, is it?"

Wynona kept her peace.

No surprise. Since Wynona had converted from a reaper to a good angel, she couldn't skirt the truth any longer, not even to spare a client's feelings. However, her eyes would reveal the sorry state of things.

Steeled for the worst, Ursula peeked through her fingers.

Wynona grinned at her smartphone screen. Her thumbs flew over the keyboard.

Ursula gritted her teeth. "Tell Rafael I said hi." After all, she and he had been going together when he'd dumped her for Wynona.

Her gaze inched up, pale cheeks flushing. Not from embarrassment...arousal. Her glazed eyes were a dead giveaway. She killed her goofy look, texted fast then put her phone, screen side down, on the treatment table. Brutal leather restraints hung from the arm and leg rests. Someone, or something, slammed into the wall behind them, followed by an unholy hiss.

Wynona arched her slender eyebrows. "How's it going?"

Scratching noises flowed from the room on the other side. Sounded like a were trying to claw through the wall to escape the ghastly treatment awaiting him. Ursula understood his pain. "You tell me. I still don't look, act or think like you."

Wynona was perfect in the looks department and blithely uninhibited around men, especially Rafael. Although tall and slender, she had enviable curves, like a Victoria's Secret model, her ample bosom not drooping as Ursula's did, her long legs fueling men's sinful dreams. Tonight, she wore a leather outfit, as usual, this one a deep rust shade. The long-sleeved top stopped beneath her breasts to reveal a creamy expanse of her torso. The band on her snug skirt grazed her navel. Her waist-length hair was white, her eyes silvery, her features exquisite.

Ursula hung her head. "I'd settle for being a millionth of what you are. You don't even get the frizzies when the weather's bad."

Rain drummed the roof and windows. The air was soupier than normal in the French Quarter and kinked Ursula's hair.

Wynona flicked her hand dismissively. Her lavender fragrance, sweet yet sultry, wafted close. "No way am I special. The way I look has zero to do with magic. Like other women, particularly mortals, I use industrial-strength conditioner available at any Walgreens. By the way, don't waste your dough on generic junk. Pantene kicks serious ass."

"If I rub it all over me, will I be like you?" *Sexy and confident, able to use bad words, indulge in indecent thoughts and get a hot guy?*

"You want to be the best of who you are, sweetie. No one else." Wynona squeezed Ursula's knee. "That's why we're using the latest technology to help you reach your goal." She'd hooked her up to an aversion therapy machine. Whenever a drab or boring woman popped up on the computer screen, the device zapped Ursula to teach her that stuff was blah. Thus far, they'd gone through most of Dr. Amy Farrah Fowler's scenes in *The Big Bang Theory*.

Despite the electricity frying her brain cells, she still found Amy's modest skirts, plaid blouses, oversized sweaters and sensible shoes rather attractive. "I don't think this is working."

Wynona played with the dial. "Maybe it's time to increase the voltage."

"If I were human, you would have electrocuted me long ago."

"No pain, no gain, right?"

"What pain? I'm beginning to like the jolts." Flushing, she squeezed her thighs together and gestured to her lady parts between them. "Down there."

"Yeah?" Wynona regarded the device with new interest. "Better than a motorized dildo, huh?"

There was no comparison. Amazon promised to deliver her machine before Friday, along with a beige sweater similar to Amy's in the latest episode. Ursula fantasized about wearing nothing except the cashmere and blubbering in ecstasy from each savage shock. Unfortunately, that didn't solve her problem.

"I don't think this is going to work." She pulled off the electrodes stuck to her temples, neck and wrists. "Let's cut through this other stuff and go for magic. A potion or spell to make me like you. Several if that's what I need."

"I'm flattered, but, no. The only way your makeover will succeed is for you to do the work, beginning with an attitude adjustment."

The were in the next room howled then panted loudly. "No, no, no," he shrieked. "I don't wanna!"

"Too bad," the staffer growled. "Get on the damn table."

"No. I—"

His scream cut off his protest. Other rooms pulsed with client moans and wails. Enforcers ran down the hall, shouting oaths and ordering customers to behave.

Ursula grabbed Wynona's soft, delicate hands. Even her knuckles were amazing. "Why can't we take a shortcut with this? Are you afraid that when I'm like you, I'll try to take Rafael away?"

Wynona turned her wrists and dug her nails into Ursula's palms. "Were you planning on doing that?"

Not any longer. She bit back a wince at the pain. "No."

Wynona released her. "You do realize potions and spells come with their own problems, right? It's like modern medicine. Ever see commercials for the newest wonder drugs? They'll cure insomnia, depression, rashes, shitty personalities, whatever, but they may also make you go blind, shrivel your lungs, stop your heart or keep you from swallowing for the rest of your life, which makes your initial complaint seem pretty tame in comparison."

"Shouldn't magic be more precise by calling on the dark powers?"

"What dark powers? All we have is Becca." Wynona scooted her chair closer and leaned in. "When Daemon wanted to ditch his satyr legs and hooves to look totally human, Becca forgot to give him feet until Heather had a meltdown."

Ursula pressed her hand to her chest. Heather was a good fairy and healer who worked as the receptionist here. Daemon, her boyfriend, was on the enforcement team. "Does Becca usually forget stuff like that?"

"Let's just say she's not the best witch on planet Earth. Before she and Eric got together, she gave him a potion that made him bald, rather than releasing his inner beast to turn him into a bad boy. Poor guy thought he was too nice, which made him lose the babes."

"He wanted other women, not her, so she made him bald?"

"What? No! Since she's lousy at spells and potions, she asked for her mom's help. Rowena's first-rate but warned magic could have unknown effects, especially on a minor god like him. Thankfully, everything worked out, but you don't want to go through that." She patted Ursula's shoulder. "A guy should love you for who you are, not who you think you want to be."

Easy for her to say. Rafael had been Wynona's parole officer when she'd been a rebel reaper, snatching souls before their time. Rather than keeping her on the straight and narrow, he'd begged her to corrupt him and had been willing to give up Heaven, his white wings and future for her. Nothing mattered, except having her love.

Ursula ached with envy. Paradise was nice but nothing without a guy to share the good stuff with. "You didn't have to change for Rafael because you're perfect. I'm not. No one's going to like me as I am."

"You're wrong. Rafael wanted me despite my faults." She shrugged. "We just clicked."

"You knew right away you were right for each other?"

"We both fought it, but yeah. You know when it fits."

She figured clicking and knowing weren't in her future since men never noticed her. If she wanted even a zillionth of what Wynona had, she'd have to be bold. "I'd like to try magic. I don't want to waste another minute."

"You haven't been at this that long." She fiddled with the machine and zapped herself lightly. A throaty hum poured from her followed by a breathless sigh and goofy grin. "Give it a chance. You have vacation time saved up."

Fifty years to be precise, since she'd never taken an hour off from her admin job in Heaven. She stood. "No. I'm going to talk to Becca."

Wynona tapped her foot, a sure sign she was frustrated, but she inhaled deeply and calmed. "I'll have a word with her. Go on, sit. I'll be back as soon as I can."

She reached the door, pivoted and returned for her smartphone. Too bad. Ursula had wanted to read Rafael's comments. She suspected they were filled with fire and passion. Perhaps a few naughty words, too. Nothing like his former bland relationship with her.

Their dates and bed-play had been more well-mannered than a senior citizens' mixer.

She'd always believed he'd been that way with her because he was an honorable man. After all, he'd earned his wings by keeping two children from drowning during Roman times and had lost his own life in the rescue. To save their pet dog, no less. What other guy would have done so for an animal that wasn't even his? Although he was better looking than the male models on romance novel covers, his allure had never made him pushy or bold during their time together. They'd kissed without exchanging tongues, made love missionary-style with the lights off and always kept most of their clothes on.

Their physical encounters were all she knew about sex. As far as their mild emotional connection went, she'd thought that was the way things should be between a woman and a man.

Then he'd met Wynona, released his beast and threatened to leave Heaven if he couldn't have her carnally and tenderly, making their souls one for eternity.

That put the kibosh on his and Ursula's limp courtship. Even if he'd still wanted her, his so-so passion wasn't enough any longer. She hungered for a man who'd turn her inside out and who would afford her unleashed desire, at least for a little while.

In preparation for her change from drab to dynamite, she googled women's leather outfits. The skirts looked too tight and the tops downright uncomfortable. However, if this was the price for a good time, so be it. She filled her Amazon cart.

"Hey, how you doin'?" The male voice rumbled like quiet thunder past the closed door.

Something inside her fluttered. She lifted her face.

In the hall, scuffles broke out. Something slammed against the door and other places, rattling the framed business license hanging above the desk.

A woman moaned.

The same male voice grunted lewdly.

"Hey!" Daemon's shout didn't stop the lusty noises. The sounds traveled to the right and grew fainter.

Footfalls bounded past.

Ursula hurried into the hall. At the far end, Heather was pressed against a door, her arms flailing. A tall man snuggled into her and sucked her throat. Given her rounded eyes and bared teeth, she wasn't loving it.

"Dammit, get away from her." Daemon grabbed the guy's arm. "She belongs to me."

Ursula had never heard a more romantic declaration.

The other man flicked Daemon off like a pesky gnat, which sent him flying backward. He bounced off the wall and dropped to the floor face down, his black shirt and pants askew.

Heather yelped. "You hurt him. How could you?" She kneed the guy.

He gasped and cradled his injured groin.

Her complexion went even paler. "I'm so sorry." She bounced on her heels and flapped her hands. "I shouldn't have done that. I'm so sorry."

Daemon groaned.

She shoved the guy away and darted past, white blouse and skirt bobbing. Her baby powder scent filled the space. Upon reaching Daemon's side, she dropped to her knees.

Heat radiated from the other man, as welcome on this cool, clammy night as hot chocolate was during a snowstorm.

Unable to help herself, Ursula edged closer.

His hair was thick and wavy. The dark brown locks tumbled over his forehead and curled around his ears. Classical Greek features made him movie-star handsome. Dark stubble dusted his firm jaw, upper lip and cheeks.

Warmth flooded her.

She had an insane urge to cup his beautiful face and stroke his bronze skin. Both were impossibly virile, the same as his broad shoulders and muscular arms. A black tee hugged his firm pecs, ripped abs and bruising biceps. He had a tribal tattoo on the right one that mesmerized her. Her nipples tightened.

His low-slung jeans left nothing to the imagination. He stopped cupping himself and revealed the enormous bulge behind his fly.

Her mouth got even drier.

"Tell me where Farron hurt you." Heather touched Daemon as a blind woman would, lingering on every spot, especially the X-rated ones. Color flooded her cheeks. Desire welled in her eyes. "I'll make it better."

The guy, Farron, snorted and made a beeline for them.

Ursula blocked him.

He reared back. Surprise crossed his features at her presence and interference. Confusion replaced it.

What could she say? She had no idea why she'd stopped him except it seemed the right thing to do. Not for Heather or Daemon, for her.

She pushed to her toes and craned her neck to drink in his straight nose, slightly flared nostrils and full mouth. Far too often, she'd dreamed of lips like his, despite the danger carnal thoughts posed to a good angel. Although her soul was pure, she was also a woman and indulged in his animal magnetism. In human years, he was probably thirty or so.

Supernaturally, he was a demon and had likely been around since time began. Tiny flames flickered in his black eyes. His scent was of the Earth and its deepest depths. The sulfur smell alone should have warned her off. Instead, his fragrance drew her to him, the same as his heat.

A zombie groaned in the room behind him.

He didn't bother looking over, regarding her instead. He frowned. "What?"

If she could have formed words, she would have introduced herself. Unfortunately, she didn't have enough strength left to smile. Drooling was her sole option.

"What the hell?" Stefin, a beefy Russian with blond hair, rushed down the hall, followed by redheaded Taro then Anatol, who sported long dreadlocks as dark as his complexion. All three were demons and enforcers there who kept clients from getting too frisky. They, like Daemon, wore black shirts and pants.

Farron grinned at the trio. His smile carved deep dimples in both cheeks, making him even more adorable.

Her legs wavered.

"Loosen up." He gave the guys a careless shrug. "I was only having a little fun."

"Not with Heather, you don't." Daemon slung his arm around her and planted his hand smack on her breast.

She turned bright pink but sagged against him.

Farron gestured in surrender. "Fine with me. Which room is mine?" He pivoted away and almost fell over Ursula.

She lifted her face to his.

He stepped back.

Stefin joined him. "I'm in charge here." He slammed his fist into his chest, his muscles thick like his accent. Taro and Anatol rolled their eyes. Stefin glared at Farron. "You'll go to the room I tell you to go to."

"Is that so?" Farron lifted his hand.

Stefin and the other demons did the same.

Power from the dark side zoomed between them.

Ursula skittered out of harm's way.

Lights flickered. Air sizzled. Farron held his own against the guys, the battle a Mexican standoff.

He laughed. A booming sound filled with mischief and surprising joy.

Enthralled, Ursula staggered toward him.

He looked over.

Taro hurled a new blast, a mega flash that turned everything blinding white. Once colors bled back in, an invisible force pinned Farron's arms to his sides. His large feet dangled several inches above the floor.

"In there." Stefin gulped air and inclined his head to the left. Together, he and the guys used their powers to push Farron into the room, his back to it.

She followed.

He stared at her, eyes widened. "*What*?"

Before she could manage a word, Anatol slammed the door and locked it. She could have walked through the barrier, an easy thing for a good angel, but that would have been rude. Disappointed, she slouched against the wall.

"Ah, guys, get a room, all right?" Wynona shook her head at Heather and Daemon making out on the floor more passionately than most couples did in bed. She stepped around them and strode to Ursula. "What are you doing out here?"

She opened her mouth but still couldn't speak.

Wynona eyed her. "Are you okay?"

Uncertain, Ursula turned to Farron's room. It was eerily quiet, considering four uncivilized males lurked inside.

"What happened to your hair?"

At Wynona's question, Ursula patted her bun, surprised to find it twice its normal size. The rest of her slicked-back do was also frizzed and poofy.

"I'll write down the name of the Pantene conditioner I use and give you an online coupon I found. Come on." Wynona steered her back into the treatment room and shut the door. "Okay, I talked to Becca. And she—"

"Who is he?"

"—agrees with me. Wait. What? Who is who?"

"The guy Anatol, Taro and Stefin hauled into the treatment room." She jabbed her thumb in that direction. "His name's Farron. Who is he? What's his story?"

"Why?"

Heat poured through Ursula. Her face burned as it never had during her time on Earth and in Heaven. "I want him."

He is the one. We fit.

Rarely had Farron been as unsettled, which surprised him.

After his literal fall from grace, he'd spent eons in Hell with nothing fazing him. Not the brimstone, heat or Satan's constant bitching about how the Big Guy, aka God, refused to see another point of view and had booted S out, leaving him nowhere to go except Hell where even the most fervent masochist would feel put upon. Yeah, yeah, yeah. Farron had heard it all, nodded agreeably and made the best of things, which included having wicked fun twenty-four-seven. Messing with people's heads was a delight. Screwing with women…

Fuck, there wasn't much to compete with that. Except a new challenge. Something to make his balls and cock sing.

He couldn't tear his attention from the hall. Given the sounds, Heather and Daemon were going at each other like wild animals, their cooing punctuated by indecent moans and grunts.

Farron had hoped she'd taste sweeter than she had, being a good fairy and all. Oddly enough, her innocence hadn't stirred him as he'd expected. What a bummer. He'd come here to tame his beast so he could meet virtuous babes, mortal or otherwise, for a change of pace. In Hell, there were no shrinking violets. If those ladies wanted a ride, they'd jump him without pause, apology or regret. He did the same with them. After an eternity filled with excess, getting it on with someone reserved sounded rather exciting.

Not Heather, though. She'd been so cool within his embrace he'd had trouble keeping warm. A first since his banishment. Her kneeing his nuts hadn't stoked his lust, either. His boys still ached, yet his rod stood at full-attention and tilted toward the hall.

Taro finished restraining Farron with the leather straps on the treatment table, after which Anatol added a powerful force field.

Stefin rocked on his heels. "Dare to make a move and we'll leave you here forever."

"Yeah?" Farron broke through the left restraint and scratched his nose.

Growling, Stefin wrestled Farron's arm down and held it while the others secured the strap. Farron twisted his right wrist, eager to pop loose from that restraint.

"I don't think so." Despite his lilting French accent and mild manner, Anatol held his fist over Farron's groin. "Stay put or I'll crack your nuts. None of us will let Heather fix them, either."

As a healer, she mended customers' physical problems at the service.

Taro chuckled. "I doubt she'd want to touch that part of him."

He had a point. She hadn't liked his tongue skimming her lips, wanting inside her mouth. For a few seconds, he'd worried she'd unclench her teeth and bite the tip off. The same reaction he'd gotten from mortal babes when he'd gotten too playful. Their response he was beginning to understand. However, what else had happened in the hall bewildered him. "Who is she?"

Stefin scratched his underarm. "A good fairy. Isn't that obvious with her white clothes, blonde hair, pale complexion and constant apologies?"

"Not Heather. The chick who was in the hall with us."

Stefin made a face. "What chick? You mean like baby poultry?" He bumped Anatol's arm. "Is Constance having one of her voodoo ceremonies tonight?"

"I think he means a woman, not a chicken."

"Ding, ding, ding." Farron smiled at Anatol. "You win the prize. So who is she?"

"I didn't see anyone." He glanced at Taro. "You?"

"Not me. You?"

Stefin shook his head.

Holy fuck, she'd been there, big as life, staring, putting him off his game and allowing the three stooges to get the upper-hand. "I almost fell over her. She's about five-five, light brown hair pulled back, no makeup, and wore a tan business suit with a white, high-necked blouse, long skirt and yukky shoes like nurses or old ladies prefer. I can't say for sure — given all she had on — but she seems to have a great rack, nice flare to her hips too. Smells clean, kind of soapy, you know? Her eyes are hazel, more on the golden side than brown. She has long, dark lashes, a creamy complexion with a touch of pink in her cheeks and her face is on the sweet-pretty side, rather than beautiful. If I had to guess, I'd say she's early to mid-twenties in human years."

The guys traded glances.

Farron wasn't surprised. He hadn't realized he'd noticed so much about her. His uneasiness returned, worrying him that kissing Heather had screwed with his brain, putting chaste desires there rather than his usual X-rated ones. The woman he'd seen certainly wasn't a *Hustler* centerfold. "You guys honestly didn't notice another female out there dressed like a missionary or one of the Duggars?"

Stefin grabbed a clipboard. "The last time I saw anyone who looked like that was when Ursula came in for her appointment."

Ech, what a name. Sounded like a parochial school teacher. "She's a nun? A demon possessed her and the service is trying to draw the evil one out?"

Maybe that's why she'd stared. She still felt the treatment effects.

Taro leaned against the counter. "Ursula was Rafael's main squeeze until he met Wynona, who used to be a reaper, but now she's a good angel like him, but only after she tried to put him off with Olaf, who's a reaper, too."

"Wait." Anatol put up his hand. "Rafael thought she was using Olaf to make him jealous after he pissed her off by kissing her and saying Becca told him to do so."

"I haven't a clue how Olaf fits into this." Taro spoke to Farron. "As far as getting Rafael to leave her be, so he wouldn't corrupt himself, Wynona asked Becca to mix a potion to turn his black wings white again. She wouldn't without his consent. I reckon we're all grateful for that, since her piss-poor potion probably would have given him another head. Constance wouldn't help, either, said it was against industry standards for her to remove his memories of Wynona without him knowing about it. No dice with MJ, too, who insisted on a contract signed in triplicate before she granted any wishes. Heather, being Heather, was too afraid to do anything she considered wrong, including healing his fucked-up wings, which pretty much left Wynona with no choice except to get down and dirty with Rafael until Frank found out and paid a visit to put a stop to that shit, which, oddly enough, had Wynona getting white wings instead of her black ones."

This was worse than trying to follow a plot on *Nashville*. Taro's country-western accent was as bad as the characters' twangs on the show. "And that makes Ursula…"

"Screwed." Stefin pointed his pen. "Though not literally."

"Yeah, I get that. Was Rafael once her guardian angel? She's mortal and he saved her life or soul or something and they got together then?"

They laughed.

Stefin wrote on his clipboard. "She's a good angel, like Rafael. Actually, better than him, never doing anything wrong, no bad thoughts, no fun, dull as dirt, totally forgettable."

Farron got that, too, since they hadn't noticed Ursula. He had, big-time, and so had his cock. The dumb thing twitched and pointed at the hall, where he'd last seen her.

Chapter Two

Ursula slumped in a break room chair and waited for the fallout. She'd been foolish to have said anything to Wynona about Farron. Stefin, Taro and Anatol still had him trapped in a treatment room, while she was stuck here.

Heather sat to her right with MJ, aka Mistress Jin, between them. Tiny bells graced the genie's wrists and ankles, tinkling each time she moved. How she could sit or walk in her super-tight jeans mystified Ursula. The denim looked painted on and should have cut off her circulation. Her lavender silk blouse had several undone buttons, which revealed her lacy black bra, the cups cut perilously low. MJ's scandalous outfit, coupled with her caramel complexion, incredible violet eyes, exotic features and wavy black hair, made her a walking billboard for female sensuality.

She bumped Heather's arm and showed her something on her smartphone.

Heather blushed. "Oh, I don't know. You don't think that's too much?"

"Let's find out." A pop sounded. Instantaneously, Heather wore a black leather cincher, arm bands and ones on her wrists. Nothing else. Brutal leather locks decorated the ensemble.

MJ gave it two thumbs-up. "Awesome, right?"

"Knock it off." Zoe, a reformed demon and the enforcers' manager, rapped her knuckles against the table. Although she barely topped five feet without high heels, she was still commanding, and dressed for success in a cream blouse, tailored brown pants and Jimmy Choo pumps. "This isn't a BDSM club." Her voice rasped deeper than James Earl Jones's — his from testosterone, hers from losing her soul long ago.

MJ smiled slyly. "The last time you and your guys were in here, you forgot something." She gestured to a red satin bra tacked to the bulletin board.

Smoke rose from Zoe's dark hair and shoulders. An occurrence that happened every time she was irritated. She batted at the sulfur-scented plumes. "Stefin did that as a joke."

He, Taro and Anatol were her lovers. On any given day, one might find them frolicking in here, playing Adam to her Eve, like in the Garden of Eden.

MJ snickered. "If you say so."

The flames in Zoe's dark eyes flared. A blush tinted her snowy skin.

"Ah, about this." Heather gestured to her non-outfit and near nudity.

A new pop filled the room. Dressed as she had been, Heather sagged against the chair. "You were right. I think that piece might work after hours."

She and MJ giggled.

Constance breezed inside. Her long apricot-colored gown made her ebony complexion richer and even more attractive. Rings on each finger twinkled in the harsh fluorescent light. The large engagement diamond on her left hand sparkled the most. "Okay, I'm here. What's this meeting about? I have a panicked zombie who wants to forget everything about his last session." The moment Constance laid her hands on anyone's skull, their memories evaporated.

Wynona inclined her head. "This is about Ursula."

"Yeah?" Constance gave her an approving smile. "What'd you do, hon?"

Nothing that she wanted to, at least not yet. "This isn't necessary."

"Becca thinks it is." Wynona stood sentinel at the door. "Soon as she gets here, we'll get started."

Constance dropped into her seat. Her spicy floral scent perfumed the air.

Daemon ran up.

Wynona pushed out her hand, barring him entrance. "Sorry. Girls only for the next few hours."

Ursula drew in her shoulders. This was worse than ancient times with their epic inquisitions.

"I'm only here for my snack." Daemon glanced past Wynona to Heather. "Can you toss it to me, babe?"

She hauled the heavy sack to him. "Enjoy."

"I will." He gave her a quick kiss and shook the monstrous bag. "Did you remember to pack Milky Ways?"

Heather rushed to the fridge, pulled out two boxes and delivered them. "This should hold you for an hour."

"If not, I'll make a run to Mickey D's." He raced away.

Constance drummed the table, her sour look on Heather. "Did you have to give him every last one of those candy bars? What are we going to eat?"

"What would you like?" MJ bowed from the waist. "You command, I obey."

From what Ursula had observed, that comment wasn't entirely true. As a genie, MJ did provide client wishes for a small fee. Although staff didn't have to pay, they did have to be careful in what they asked for. MJ had a mischievous streak as long as China's Great Wall. Every time Daemon asked for a Busch, as in beer, she delivered shrubs, as in bushes. A private joke that made her double over with laughter.

Heather stroked MJ's arm. "Be nice, okay?"

"Anything for you." A faint pop sounded. Chocolate candy littered the table. Deli meats, cheeses and side dishes filled the counters.

Everyone dug in.

Ursula couldn't, wanting to hurl.

Becca stood in the doorway. Black eyeshadow ringed her lids and made her irises seem implausibly blue. The color matched the silky crop top and harem pants draping her generous curves. Maroon lipstick completed her Goth makeup. Like Zoe, she was super pale, which somehow went well with her flame-colored bob. She wore dangling navel jewelry, anklets, toe rings and a spectacular diamond on her left finger, the engagement stone as large as the one Constance sported.

Clearly, Eric had gotten over her previous faux pas in making him bald.

She swung the door closed, locked it and honed in on Ursula. "What are you thinking?"

Everyone's gaze swung to her. She pressed into her chair. "Only that I don't like you ganging up on me."

"This is an intervention." Wynona held a plate heaped with roast beef, potato salad and slaw. She pulled up a chair. "Trust me, you need help."

Not true. She craved passion and love like they were getting, especially Zoe. She had more than one partner and no one hollered at her. "I know what I'm doing."

Constance peeled the wrapper from her Milky Way. "What exactly are you doing?"

"Nothing except sitting here and breathing."

"Wrong." Wynona pointed her fork. "You want Farron."

"What?" Constance gaped. "Have you even met him?"

"Not formally, but when we were in the hall—"

"Wait. Don't tell me. Before you could blink, he said 'How you doin'?' like Joey in *Friends* then he was all over you."

"Not really." Her cheeks got hot. "He was all over Heather."

She covered her face. "It was awful. I couldn't get him to leave me alone."

"Exactly." Constance frowned at Ursula. "The first time I saw him, he practically tackled me. That's the way he is. He sees a woman and boom, he's on her faster than a fly on honey."

He hadn't been that way with her. Of course, he'd been busy battling Taro, Anatol and Stefin. They had been a major distraction. "He doesn't seem that bad."

Constance's eyes bugged out. She twisted in her chair to speak to Becca. "Did you tell her that he'd be civilized after his treatments like you did with me?" She turned back. "Don't believe that for a minute. He's never going to be different. He's been coming here forever. If anything, he's worse than when he first came to this place."

"We're making some progress." Becca crossed the room and stopped at Ursula's chair. "That doesn't mean you should have any interest in him. He's way beyond anything you could handle. Even MJ would have trouble with him."

MJ bit into her ham and Swiss on rye, bells jingling. "Not my type. Wynona can have him."

"Gee, thanks." After smearing Dijon on her beef, Wynona slathered on mayo. "If he was human, his soul would've been toast a long time ago. My reaping him would have been a public service."

"No kidding, but even Hell doesn't want him." Zoe worked her tongue around her mouth and swallowed. "Rumor has it, he gives S no end of shit."

Constance bumped her arm. "And you didn't?"

They laughed.

Ursula bounced in her chair. "This isn't funny."

Zoe swallowed her soda. "We're not laughing at you, but at S."

She didn't understand. "Who or what is that?"

"Satan. We call him S for short. Sometimes, I refer to him as TT for The Turd. That SOB put one over on me to get my soul. I can't begin to tell you how he—"

"Wait." As a rule, Ursula wasn't this bold, but she didn't have a choice. "I thought we were talking about me. No matter what anyone says against Farron, I want him."

Everyone stopped eating and fell silent. Even the rowdy clients had paused for a breather.

Becca hunkered down at her side. "Why, for God's sake?"

His great looks, awesome bod, killer dimples and wondrous laugh came to mind, along with the fact he was the one. He'd actually noticed her, stared back and asked "What?" repeatedly when she'd been invisible to the other guys. Whether Farron would harbor anything for her except morbid curiosity or caution, was another matter. She might have to settle for what the ladies called wild monkey sex, which she supposed included positions other than missionary, making love with the lights on and possibly being nude.

"The usual reasons." Her cheeks stung.

Becca lowered her face and groaned. "This can't be happening."

"It's okay." Ursula patted her head. "I know what I'm doing."

"Sure." Zoe popped a Dove miniature into her mouth. "Have you forgotten he's a demon and you're a good angel?"

"So? Wynona was a reaper and Rafael wasn't only a good angel—he was her parole officer when they met. I didn't see that stopping them. In Heaven, we viewed the video from their night at The Thin Red Line and the Double B room that someone put on Facebook." Never in her existence had she observed such sexual depravity or knew Rafael's smile could be so wide and blissful.

Wynona sniffed. "You're mixing apples with oranges. We both served Heaven."

"Before, after or while you were corrupting him?"

She grinned dreamily. "If you think I'm going to apologize or feel bad about that, no fucking way. He asked. I complied. Everything worked out."

"The same as it will with me and Farron."

"Not exactly." Becca stood and clamped her hand on Ursula's shoulder, her grip hard enough to leave a bruise.

She winced.

Becca leaned in. "No way is Heaven going to go for this. You and Farron are at opposite ends of the spectrum, serving different masters who happen to loathe each other. Their ongoing battle is worse than the Hatfields and the McCoys."

Heather straightened. "Or Taylor Swift and Katy Perry."

"Try the Jenners and Kardashians." Zoe made a face. "What I've read in the *Enquirer* about them." She shook her head.

"Kris kind of had a point in being upset." MJ glanced around the table. "But I understand Caitlyn's point of view, too. You gotta be who you are, you know?"

"That's what I'm trying to tell you." Ursula gestured helplessly. "I'm simply going with my feelings."

Becca dug harder. "You're not thinking straight. Once you finish your treatments, Wynona will set you up with a nice guy. Another good angel, right?"

"Sure. A real cutie." She winked.

Ursula pushed Becca's hand off and stood. "I want Farron. I don't care if he hurts me, as long as I get a smidge of what you guys have. So far today, Heather's necked with Daemon in front of me and everyone else. I'm sure after our meeting, Zoe will invite the guys in here for one of their afternoon delights." She pointed at Wynona. "You have my old boyfriend." She swung her finger to Becca. "You're engaged to a minor god, rather than a warlock, who would be more fitting for a witch, even a half-mortal one. And how about you?" She focused on Constance. "Is your guy a voodoo priest to match up with you being a voodoo priestess?"

"Try a NOLA cop." Zoe shot Constance a hard look. "Talk about giving us the proverbial heart attack when you told him to come here—to check us out—then begged us to be normal so he wouldn't know what was really going on."

"Hold it." Ursula's inherent caution jacked up a notch. "Why would you have to hide anything? Are you doing something illegal here?"

Becca smiled wanly. "Paranormal. Gabe's mortal."

She sucked in a breath. "And you have the gall to tell me I shouldn't be with a demon?"

Becca pushed her back to the chair. "You bet. Gabe's not damned to Hell like Farron is. If anything does happen between you two, how would you work things out? There's nowhere you'll both belong. Heaven will certainly be off-limits to you once you're corrupted and your wings have turned black like Rafael's did after he hooked up with Wynona. Thankfully, Frank, Rafael's boss, gave them an out by letting her become a good angel. Which only leaves Satan to help you. Even if he doesn't mind you being on his turf, I'm guessing you're not going to like sin city one damn bit. If nothing else, I hear the heat is hell."

"Don't knock it till you've tried it." The flames in Zoe's pupils flashed. "The SC clubs are epic."

Ursula shook her head. "SC?"

"Second Circle—lust."

Everyone had answered as one.

A jolt from Wynona's aversion therapy machine couldn't have aroused Ursula as much. She squirmed in her chair, trying to relieve the pleasant ache between her legs. "Tell me everything."

"Not one word, I mean it." Becca scowled at Zoe then spoke to Ursula. "All I'm asking is that you consider what you're doing. When things don't work out—"

"When, not if?"

"Fine. *If* things don't work out, you won't be able to ever go home to Heaven because of your tainted wings, not to mention whatever else his loving might do to you."

Warmth burst within her chest and traveled past her torso to her stomach, creating an incredibly pleasant feeling. Whatever Farron wanted to do to her and with her, she was game. Besides, what Becca had asserted wasn't entirely true. "If we break up and my wings or other parts are a mess, why can't Heather heal them and me? Or I could ask for a wish to make everything better. Right, MJ?"

"Maybe." She licked crumbs off her lips. "*Everything* might technically be more than one wish. I'd have to check. But, hey, if you have the bucks and sign a contract in triplicate, you bet."

Sounded good to her. "Heather? How about you? Would you help heal me?"

She squirmed. "If that's what you want, I guess I could try."

"Thanks." Ursula smiled at Becca. "Looks like I'm covered."

"Don't be so sure. What if MJ's and Heather's powers don't work? Are you prepared to lose everything you've worked for, all you've known, the people you consider your family and friends for one lousy roll in the hay with Farron?"

"I was hoping it would be good, not horrible, and would happen more than one time." It simply had to.

Becca shoved her bangs off her forehead. "I'm speaking metaphorically. Unless you're willing to give up everything for him, don't do this."

It would be more wrong for her not to try. "Did you think that way when you fell for your minor god or Constance with her mortal cop or Wynona with her good angel parole officer? I think not." Ursula stood. "I'm through talking."

Her throat was too tight to speak. Tears also threatened. She grabbed a napkin and felt tip marker from the counter then printed the last thing she would have said if they had urged her on and cheered her decision to go forward, rather than telling her she was nuts.

Maybe she was, but after an eternity of blah, she wanted to live. By gosh, she was going to. Emboldened, she held the napkin above her head.

Constance read aloud. "The soul wants equality for all."

"How beautiful." Heather pressed her hands to her chest.

Becca shook her head.

"Hey, you know who Ursula reminds me of?" Zoe glanced at the others. "Sally Field in *Norma Rae* when she'd had it with the factory where she worked and held a paper with the word *union* above her head."

"Right." Constance smiled. "Great movie. One of Sally's best."

"*Forrest Gump* was as good."

"What about *Steel Magnolias*?" Wynona sighed. "My personal fave."

Several ladies agreed and offered other film titles. Everyone spoke at once, exchanging comments and laughs.

As they debated Sally's worst movies, including *Smokey and the Bandit*, Ursula gobbled Milky Ways, Mars bars and Dove candies. Hard liquor would have been better, but she hoped a sugar rush would give her the courage to do what her feelings required, despite Becca's stony gaze.

* * * *

Farron eyed his tormentors. "You're sure about this?"

Stefin and the others had bypassed the usual behavior modification to try something different with him. Aversion therapy and what they called targeting the real problem, Farron's family jewels.

Stefin smiled. "If your junk don't work no more, you can't scare away women with it, can you?"

If he couldn't get it up any longer, there'd be no reason to exist. "What are you talking about? I will be able to use my cock after this, right?"

"In most instances."

Sweat broke out on his forehead. "How about in those situations I'm counting on? Like when I'm with a babe? And how soon can I expect to get back to normal?"

"Define normal."

He clenched his jaw so hard his neck ached. "How. Fucking. Soon?"

"We don't like to promise."

"I've changed my mind." Farron pushed up and fell back, the restraints and force fields surprisingly sturdy. He didn't want to beg, but… "Come on, let me loose."

Stefin laughed. "Relax, I'm yanking your chain. You'll be fine. Don't you want to restrain your beast so you don't run women off?"

That was the least of his worries. "How's this treatment supposed to work?"

"If you have any impure thoughts, the machine will know."

I'm a dead man. "What'll it do?"

"Keep you focused on control." He pasted electrodes to Farron's balls. Anatol and Taro shoved a penis extender on his rod.

Having another inch or two to wow the ladies excited Farron.

The guys tightened and pulled the extender fucking hard.

His nuts shriveled. He gritted his teeth at the pain. The only thing that would ease it would be a woman's mouth on him. Maybe Ursula's.

Several electrical jolts raged through the electrodes to his sac.

White-hot agony exploded every-fucking-where. He flopped on the treatment table, gagged and possibly screamed. His balls bloated faster than a rotting corpse.

Daemon sauntered in, chocolate smears on his mouth, crumbs dotting his black shirt. He swallowed and belched. "How's he doing?"

Farron had yet to catch his breath and panted like a dying dog.

Stefin wiggled his eyebrows. "Almost fainted."

"Good." Daemon pushed his face into Farron's. "Stay away from Heather."

She was the furthest thing from his mind. Ursula kept invading his thoughts, especially the way she'd stared, wonder and arousal mingled on her pretty face. He bet her nipples had peaked and her pussy had creamed.

A new jolt blasted from the electrodes to him, rattling his molars. He tried to form words. They came out garbled.

Stefin cupped his ear. "What was that?"

It took Farron several tries before he could form coherent words. "Take this fucking thing off me. I didn't mean to do what I did in the hall. I'm sorry. I lost my head."

"You'll lose more than that if you don't behave." Anatol flipped a page on the chart. "We'll throw in castration free of charge."

"I'll be good." He could scarcely breathe but had to reason with Daemon. "If these pricks hurt my stuff accidentally, will Heather heal me?"

He shoved a Quarter Pounder with cheese into his mouth and swallowed it whole. "Nope."

"The machine can handle him from now on." Stefin gestured the others to the door. "Looks like we're through here."

"Hey, wait." Farron lifted his head. A muscle pulled. He gasped. "How long will this last?"

"Forever, if the treatment works. If it doesn't, we'll have to neuter you." Laughing, he and the guys left.

No matter how much dark power Farron used, he couldn't yank free. Hyperventilating, he drooped to the table. Perspiration ran down his face and chest. Terrorized at having to endure more misery, he kept his thoughts pure.

Light footfalls sounded in the hall. Rather than pass, they neared his door.

Ursula. Her clean, soapy scent wafted into the room.

He liked her gold-brown eyes, velvety skin, pink lips and the small mole near her temple. Her puffy hair was a bit strange, but it didn't bother him any more than her matronly clothes and butt-ugly shoes had. Once she was stripped bare, her female assets would only add to her allure.

Defying all odds, his cock grew rigid and thick.

The machine zinged his nuts three times in rapid succession, each shock more powerful than the last. Everything went black.

When he came to, Farron wasn't certain how much time had passed. The rain hadn't let up, but there weren't any windows in there to check whether it was dusk or dawn. No clocks, either, and he'd never owned a watch. What was the point when he had nowhere to go with forever to get there?

To his surprise, the restraints were off, his jeans pulled up and zipped. Cautiously, he stroked his bulge, gagged at the hurt and bit back a wail. His balls ached like a sonofabitch and felt like they were three times their normal size. Murderous pain shrieked from his cock to his teeth. Shaking worse than a doomed mortal, he pushed up and swung his legs over the table. The room lurched. No way could he walk or crawl out of there. Each breath he took hurt his boys.

He called on his powers to whisk him to The Crucible, a hotspot for supernatural beings not too far from this place. To take even a second more to descend to Hell would be wasted time. He needed a liter of Hill's Absinth fast. The seventy-proof booze would blunt his misery and burn away bad memories. With the nightclub in mind, he waited for a supersonic transport.

Nothing happened.

Panicked, he focused harder but didn't budge from this godforsaken nuthouse, nor could he will the booze into existence. There had to be a reasonable explanation for his failure and he'd have it seconds before tearing out Stefin's guts. If he could gather enough steam to find the SOB.

He slid off the table and gritted his teeth at the vicious throb between his legs. Like Frankenstein's monster, he lurched to the door, froze and sniffed. Ursula's soapy smell enveloped him, stirring his cock. A bad, bad move. Pain ripped from his groin to his shoulders and dipped to his ass. Sucking air, he turned and gasped.

Ursula pushed out of the only chair in the room, her crappy clothes and poofy hair the same as the last time he'd seen her. She stared.

He tottered back. "What? For fuck's sake, talk—wait." He bunched his shoulders. "Did you steal my powers? Is this some kind of sick joke?"

"Are your powers gone?"

Her breathy sweet voice and wide-eyed look drained his rage faster than a blow to his head. "Uh…I'm not sure. I tried to zip out of here, but I can't."

"Maybe I can help."

Before she got too close, he danced back. His rod and boys screamed in agony. Sweat blurred his vision. His shoulder hit the wall. He flinched and sidled away. "What are you going to do?"

"Help you. I'm Ursula, by the way." She stuck out her hand.

Afraid to touch her, he wiggled his fingers. "Hey. How do you plan to help me? Do you know where Stefin is? The moment I get that prick between my fists, I'm going to tear out his pissing—"

"Excuse me for interrupting, but I thought we could help each other."

That didn't make sense, unless… "You're here to convert me so you get another gold star in Heaven? No fucking way. I'm not into celibacy, singing *Kumbaya* at airports or having bake sales for worthy causes. I'd have more fun watching cells divide."

She sucked her bottom lip.

His foul mood nosedived, shame replacing it. Despite his bad day, he didn't have to be such a louse. "Look, I'm sorry, but your lifestyle isn't for me. Maybe you can work on Heather. She's purer than the driven snow and boring as crap too."

"Heather's a wonderful woman."

If Ursula had kissed her as he had, she wouldn't be saying that. "Okay."

"I'm not here to convert you." She brightened. "You can stay exactly as you are. In my book, you're perfect."

He didn't believe that for a moment. "Perfect for what?"

She wrung her hands. Her cheeks got so red they practically glowed. "Me."

"Huh?"

"I know you're having trouble suppressing your beast, and since I'm —"

"Back up. How do you know why I'm here? That incident in the hall with Heather was a misunderstanding."

"I'm sure. But I read your file."

"Stefin gave it to you?"

"Oh, no. I hacked into the service's accounts while you were unconscious. I've worked in admin forever. I know all the software and can get into anything I want. Sometimes I do just to keep busy, but I never share information. Anyway, getting back to me. I'm taking treatments at the service to loosen up, get hip, make whoopee."

"Huh?"

She inched closer.

With nowhere to go, except through the wall, he stayed where he was.

She smiled gently, sweetly.

Her response and presence touched something deep inside him. His cock pulsed. Painful spasms shot up his torso and down his legs. He dug his nails into his palms to keep from yelling and crying.

"Are you all right?"

Sweat dripped in his eye. He ignored the sting. "Yep. Go on."

"Ah, I thought I could help you control your inner urges while you help me relax and have fun so we both become what we really want. Not here though. We'd have to help each other and enjoy ourselves somewhere else."

He ran her suggestion around his brain. "You want me to take you out, like on a date, then sleep with you while I restrain myself?"

"Not exactly. Be just the way you are with me, but don't pounce on other women while we're together." She beamed. "What you suggested sounds wonderful. Yes. I'd love to go on a date with you. What day and time should I be ready?"

He couldn't recall having asked her out or whether he should. "Before we get too far, you're a virgin, right?"

"No." Her throat turned hot pink. "Is that a problem?"

More like a revelation. "Why me? Aren't there any good angels you're interested in? That is, besides Rafael."

Her eyebrows shot up. "You know about him?"

"The staff gossips. You still pining for him? You plan to use me to make him jealous?"

"No. I don't play games."

He did, and a whole lot more. Even the vilest demon would know anything happening between them wasn't right. "Sorry, no can do. I don't want to be responsible for you getting hurt."

She pulled back her shoulders. Her features hardened, as a nun's would with a recalcitrant student. "I'm not a child. I can take care of myself."

"I beg to differ. You have no idea what I'm like."

"Wrong. I read your file. Shame on you for wanting to corrupt nice women simply to have a good time."

He laughed. "Oh, yeah? Haven't you listened to anything you've said? That's precisely what you want me to do to you. And by the way, I tried my charm on Heather. Talk about a cold fish. I practically got frostbite. She might be the best thing since sliced bread, but she sure as fuck isn't for me. I've finally figured out innocence doesn't heat my blood."

Her eyes shone. Her narrow shoulders trembled.

He didn't like that. "Are you about to cry?"

"No." She sniffed. "How do you know someone who's good isn't your type? You haven't tried me yet."

A tear wiggled down her cheek.

Guilt gripped him. He fought the emotion. "I'm sure you're great, but this would never work between us. Not even for a second."

"Let's find out." She slipped her fingers through his hair.

His breath caught. Her touch was exquisitely light, surprisingly heated, her scent intoxicating, any contact between them pure crazy. If she wouldn't stop this, he had to. "I-I-I—"

"Shh." She brushed her lips over his.

Delight whispered between their mouths. Her sweetly scented breath made him reel.

He grabbed her for support.

She wreathed her arms around his neck and pressed so close his junk should have ached, but didn't. He had no idea what was happening, and for some reason couldn't resist, letting her lead the way.

She kissed him tenderly.

His strength drained. Wonder and restraint replaced it. He'd always been an impatient lover, racing through foreplay, barreling toward the main attraction, then, after a few sweaty moments, breezing away to more fun and another conquest.

He couldn't move or think. Her lips were too soft to deny, her gentle regard like nothing he'd known. What he imagined a child felt from a loving parent, or a man experienced with a woman who desired no one except him, dismissing his fuck-ups, celebrating his victories, making him feel more potent than all the dark powers he owned.

Having the ability to frighten and destroy was about control. This was about…

He hadn't a clue. Scared, he should have pulled away and bolted outside.

Instead, he angled his mouth and slipped his tongue between her lips.

Chapter Three

He *was* the one.

Ursula sagged into him and wallowed in his delicious kiss. His lips searched rather than pillaged. His bristly cheeks rasped hers in the best possible way, while his heat… There weren't enough words to describe how he warmed her inside and out. From the moment she'd become a good angel, every supervisor had warned her to avoid a demon's inner fire. How even their slightest touch on someone like her would be worse than acid eating away skin.

They'd lied…or had been mistaken.

Farron's embrace comforted, aroused and enveloped her in passion she hadn't known existed. She not only accepted his tongue but invited him to explore more deeply inside her mouth. To enjoy her as she did him, despite French kissing being off-limits.

If this was wrong, she didn't want to be right. He tasted slightly metallic and all male, delightfully primitive and rough. Thrilled, she nuzzled closer.

A low growl rumbled from him. His chest vibrated against hers.

She answered his passion and sucked his tongue, eager to discover its contours. A rare feast for such a lonely being. Not once during her Earthly existence had she done anything except serve others, never considering what she might need. Those days were over.

She gripped his hair, the thick tresses softer than kitten fur. A lovely and familiar ache settled between her legs, far better than what she'd known from the aversion therapy machine or a dildo. This was the real deal.

He rocked her back and forth, deepening the kiss. Wasn't enough. In their desire to get closer, they turned circles. She bumped the table. His shoulder brushed the wall. They knocked into the chair. It rolled across the room.

He stilled at the sound, pulled his mouth free and raised his chin to the ceiling. His Adam's apple bobbed from his hard swallow.

Short, dark hairs roughened his skin. Fascinated, she licked the prominent ridge in his throat.

He shuddered and lowered his face.

His flaming eyes entranced her.

Thankfully, he looked thunderstruck rather than unhappy.

During her time in Heaven and her few years on Earth, no man had regarded her as he did now. Wasn't permitted. Those days had been awful and she refused to recall them. Only this moment mattered.

Their moisture mingled on his lips. His mouth looked as bruised as hers felt. She spoke from the heart. "Thank you."

He blinked slowly, the way one does upon awakening or emerging from a trance. "Huh?"

Brash with confidence, she touched his soft cotton tee, not as nice as skin, but wonderful, nonetheless. After another kiss, she'd hopefully have the courage to stroke his tattoo. Maybe even lick the design. "When and where?"

He released her and swayed. "What?"

"Do you need to sit?"

"No. Yeah. Maybe. Why?"

"You're wobbling right to left. Now forward and back."

He pressed his palm against the wall and lowered his head. "I'm fine."

If he kept gulping air as he did, he'd use up the oxygen in this room. "Does your ah...your um..." Unable to say the words, she gestured to his fly. "Are you in pain?"

"No. Yeah. Shit, I don't know. It hurts but not like before. That was fucking awful, yet it went away." He eyed her suspiciously. "Why?"

She lifted her shoulders. "Beats me. I don't work here." She pointed behind herself. "Want me to ask a staffer what's going on?"

"No. I don't trust them."

"Oh, you should. They're good people...most of the time."

"They're not human, which means they're not people, and clearly you've never been strapped to that thing like I was." He gestured to the treatment table. "I gotta get out of here before they come back and try more of their shit on me."

"No—wait." She touched his chest. Only granite could compete in hardness to his firm muscles. Her knees sagged and her breath spilled out. Overwhelmed, she stared.

He did too then frowned. "We're back to this? What? Spit it out. Please. I'm begging you."

"You don't have to plead." She stroked his pec. Goosebumps broke out on her arms. "When and where?"

"What are you talking about?" He caressed her hand.

Dizzy, she lowered her head.

He squeezed. "What?"

"That feels unbelievably good. Please don't stop."

He did and backed away.

She tracked him to the wall.

He bumped into it.

She pretended not to notice. "When will you be picking me up and where will we be going for our date?"

"I-I-I—"

"That's okay." She touched his lips, quieting him. Unfortunately, her gesture did nothing to calm. His color was too high, eyes bulging. In another second, he might faint or flee. "Take a few minutes to figure it out. I'm good with whatever you decide. Be as bold as you want. I'll be ready for anything."

Before he could speak, she rushed out of the door and ran into Taro.

He jumped back. So did she.

Stefin frowned. "What were you doing in there?" He strode into the room. "Stefin here— Uh-uh. You're not through. Back on the damn table."

Farron's snarl flowed into the hall. "Fuck that and you."

"Want to bet?"

"Showtime." Taro dashed inside, Anatol on his heels. The door slammed. Blazing light bled past the jamb. The atmosphere crackled.

Ursula bolted past a startled staffer and skidded to a stop at Heather's desk.

She pushed back so forcefully her chair shot straight into the potted plants behind her. Fronds hung over her head. Alarm registered on her ethereal features. "What?" She glanced at the hall. Howls and shrieks poured down it. "Is something after you?"

If she were lucky, Farron would be. "Can you do anything except heal?"

"Oh, sure." She brushed a leaf away and smiled sweetly. "I do the accounting, make and keep track of appointments, order supplies, answer phones, keep things tidy up here..." She gestured. Everything was pristine. Coral walls, faux gas fixtures and vintage furniture added a romantic touch to the cozy space and contradicted what happened in the treatment rooms. "Becca even signed me up for a computer course so I can upgrade our software when—"

"You can't help me." She flew to the next hall.

Heather called out, "Sorry."

"Not your fault." Ursula needed magic. White, dark, good, bad, she didn't care. She had to have something potent fast.

Not bothering to knock, she threw open Becca's door.

Her reddish eyebrows lifted.

Wynona glanced over from the needlepoint sofa.

Ursula slumped against the jamb. "What are you doing here?"

"We might ask you the same." Becca pushed away from her Louis XIV desk and crossed the room. "What's wrong?"

She closed and locked the door. "You have to help me."

"Finally." Wynona patted the stiff cushion next to her. "Sit. We'll talk treatment plans then I'll show you headshots of these guys Rafael knows. New recruits in Heaven. Sweet as can be. You'll love—"

"I want magic." She stormed to Becca. "Right. This. Minute. I'm willing to pay whatever you want. Money's no object." Contrary to popular belief, paradise didn't run on sugar, spice and everything nice. Cold hard currency ruled up there, the same as everywhere else. "Not only did I save up all my vacation time, I did the same with my salary. Let's get started."

"Not so fast. What did you want the potion or spell to do?"

"Help me seduce Farron."

Wynona made a pained sound and buried her face in her hands.

Undaunted, Ursula lifted her chin. "We've already kissed and I enjoyed it."

Becca gasped. "Show me your wings."

"They're fine."

"Prove it."

Grumbling, she unfurled the things. The tips touched opposite walls.

Becca scurried from side to side then hurried behind, checking. She let out a huge breath. "They're still white."

"Told you." She retracted them.

Wynona pinched her nose. "When Rafael's wings turned black from being with me, there was a delayed reaction before the change started. Could be your feathers are darkening as we speak."

She gestured dismissively. "Then I'll have MJ or Heather fix them."

"You're getting ahead of yourself." Becca regarded her. "Are you sure he kissed you? Do you know what a kiss is? I mean literally? There aren't any burn marks on your lips. They're a little puffier than I recall but not blistered."

"He's hot, not dangerous and I'm not that naïve. I know what a kiss is. Sex, too." She shrugged. "What you call the vanilla kind. But I'm willing to try new stuff, even keeping the lights on while we frolic."

Wynona moaned.

Becca rounded her desk and sat. "He didn't try anything besides kissing you? Like copping a feel, pushing you on the floor or tearing at your clothes?"

"Of course not. He was gentle and sweet."

Surprise and delight lit Becca's face. "What do you know? The treatments are working."

"Don't be so sure." Wynona crossed her legs. "It's possible he didn't do anything more because he wasn't enjoying himself." She spoke to Ursula. "I don't mean to be rude, but if your kiss went so well, why do you need magic? Didn't he like what you guys did?"

"I'm not sure. You tell me." She gave them a blow-by-blow description of what had happened.

Color drained from their faces.

Bile rose to Ursula's throat. She swallowed the gruesome taste and wanted to gag. "He hates me? He finds me repulsive? Not even magic will help?"

Wynona shook her head.

Her belly cramped. "What am I going to do if potions and spells won't work?"

"Hon, if he shoved his tongue halfway down your throat, then ended up dizzy and breathless, you don't need magic or anyone's help. You're doing fine on your own. Damn, who would've thought?"

Becca frowned. "Have you made plans with him?"

"I tried, but he couldn't relax long enough to give me an answer. He seemed scared. I thought he was going to turn me down or take off, so I rushed here. Whatever he's feeling, you have to make me look and act like a red tomato so I can seduce him before he gets a chance to think this out."

"A red what?"

"Like her." She inclined her head to Wynona and offered a pleasant smile. "I love your leather outfit. Can I borrow it for my date with Farron?"

"Only if you promise to burn it afterward."

"Stop it. He's a nice guy." She rapped Becca's desk. "Let's get started on the spell or potion. Whatever you think would work best."

Wynona stood. "Have you forgotten what I told you about Eric going bald?"

Not in the least. Desperate times called for desperate measures, even chancing a Becca potion or spell. Besides, Eric's photographs on the cabinet proved he had nice hair again. Becca had finally gotten him right and could do the same in this instance. "Magic is my only option. I don't have time for a department-store makeover or plastic surgery."

"How about a wish?"

"Wynona." Becca glared.

Ursula's spirits soared into the stratosphere. "Of course. If MJ can fix black wings, she should be able to do a makeover. Thanks." She shot to the door.

Wynona grabbed her arm and pulled her back. "Let's have her come in here. You'll need help crafting your wish so it comes out right."

"And witnesses if it doesn't." Becca made a face. "Are you absolutely certain you want to do this? Nothing will stop you?"

"Yes, to your first question. No, to the second."

With a heavy sigh, Becca punched her intercom button. "MJ, in here, pronto."

"Why? I swear the reaper wanted fangs like a vamp."

She rubbed her forehead. "We'll discuss that later. In here. Now."

Seconds after MJ arrived, Heather, Constance and Zoe streamed in. Constance wagged a bejeweled finger. "I knew this was about Ursula. What did you do this time?"

"Farron and I kissed."

Everyone except Becca and Wynona recoiled. Someday, she'd change their minds about him. For now, she needed help fast. "I have to look and act like a hot potato so I can seduce him."

Constance arched one eyebrow. "Vegetables aside, you want to seduce him after your kiss? Isn't that backwards?"

"I don't have time to go into that now. I need a wish."

All eyes shot to MJ.

Her Cheshire cat grin sent shivers through Ursula, warning her to take care. "I don't know what to say. How to do this. Someone help me, please. That's not a wish. It's a request."

"I'll handle it." Zoe clamped MJ's shoulder. "Remember when you helped me ditch my facial piercings and prissy uniform so I could snag my guys? Do the same for Ursula."

"Seriously? You want me to put her in your Debbi does Delta Psi getup? That rocked."

They snickered. Zoe sobered first. "Behave. No need to add to her misery, since wanting Farron is punishment enough."

"Hey." She tapped her foot. "He's. A. Nice. Guy."

No one agreed.

MJ stroked her throat. "Better get started."

Pops sounded. Leather outfits in every color crowded Becca's office. Lace and satin bras hung over one Tiffany lamp and scanty thongs dangled from the other.

The ladies sank to the sofa and chairs, arms and legs crossed, waiting.

Ursula figured undressing for Farron in broad daylight would be less daunting than this. "You're going to watch me?"

MJ leaned forward. "You're going to give us a show."

Constance whistled through her teeth. Wynona pumped her fist. Heather went into a full body blush. Becca lifted her gaze to the ceiling.

This was as bad as when she'd first landed in Heaven, didn't know the ropes and made stupid mistakes. Everyone snickered or traded glances that said she was too dumb to live. Her eyes filled. A tear slipped down her cheek. "Quit making fun. What happens tonight is important to me."

Their features went slack. Wynona jumped up first, followed by the others. Together they hugged her, even Zoe who was hot to the touch. Everyone swayed as Farron had. He'd felt far better, though, this was nice. Ursula never had a real family after her sixth year on Earth. Her days had revolved around endless, boring tasks then she'd died horribly and shot straight to Heaven. There, she'd made an awkward transition to a mind-numbing admin job and more denial of the woman she could have been. And might never be. "Is this going to help?"

Heather squeezed harder. "Hugging always does."

"No. I meant my makeover. Will it help?"

Wynona let go first and swiped her eyes. "When we're through, you're going to knock him on his ass."

"Oh, no. I don't want to hurt him. I just want him to like and keep seeing me, literally, like I'm actually there. Other guys haven't. I'm invisible to them."

Wynona cupped Ursula's chin. "I give you my word we won't let him hurt you."

She grabbed Wynona's wrist. "You're not going to harm him...um...down there, are you?"

"Not if you don't want me to, but we are going to protect your sweet butt. Right, guys?"

"Whatever it takes." Zoe slammed her fist into her palm. "No one messes with the ladies here."

"Come on. Time for you to shine." Wynona tugged Ursula to the first rack stuffed with outfits in kaleidoscope colors, the designs scandalous, the leather skins smelling decadent. Like a woman on a mission, Wynona rifled through the dresses, curling her upper lip at most. She looked over at MJ. "You couldn't come up with anything better than this?"

The genie smiled. A pop followed.

No new clothing appeared on the rack, lamps or other furniture.

Wynona pointed at Ursula. "Look down, hon."

She did and flinched. Her dress, if you could call it that, was blood red with wide leather straps that barely covered her bosom and other private area. She crossed her arms and legs to hide herself. "I'm not wearing this."

"No kidding." Zoe circled her. "I've had thongs with more material in them."

"MJ." Wynona clenched her jaw. "Quit. Playing. Around."

"Sorry. She wants decent, I'll give her decent." Another pop.

Ursula was in a burka with a thin veil covering her eyes. She wanted to shriek.

Heather smacked MJ's arm then gasped. "I shouldn't have done that. I'm sorry, but you need to behave. We have to help her, not drive her nuts."

Ursula sank to the sofa and rocked like the deranged. MJ sighed. "Fine."

On the next pop, Ursula squeezed her lids, afraid to look.

"Definitely better." Wynona stepped closer. "But not exactly a hot potato or a red tomato look either. We want her to stop him dead."

Curious about what she now wore, she opened her eyes. The royal blue dress was in leather, like the other garments, but had an empire waist, high neckline, full calf-length skirt and puffy sleeves. "This is cute."

Constance put a gold sheath back on the rack. "For a ten-year-old going to her first mixer with the other homeschooled kids. If you're really into Farron —"

"I am."

"Then wear black. It's pure seduction. Am I right, ladies?"

Heather lifted her shoulders. "White is nice, too, unless he's taking you to a place like Whatever Goes."

"Anything Goes, remember?" MJ wiggled her eyebrows at Ursula. "It's an epic BDSM club."

Heather blew out a sigh. "The best. The manacles, crowds, whips." She squealed softly.

Ursula couldn't recall how to breathe and was too shy to ask what BDSM stood for. She figured the whips and manacles had something to do with it, given what she'd seen in Farron's file. His proclivities had astounded and aroused. However, reading about them and actually indulging in those acts with him were worlds apart.

The room spun. She grabbed the cushions to keep steady. "Wynona, what do you think?"

"I'm with Constance. Black rules. Becca?"

Nothing.

She'd slipped away, unnoticed.

* * * *

Stefin keyed into the computer. "Only a few more questions and we're through."

Farron didn't believe the bum for a moment. Already he'd asked too much, from Farron's shoe size to how long his cock had been when they'd commandeered him into this room. To his everlasting relief, the crappy treatment hadn't shrunk him anywhere and even gave his shaft an extra inch.

Unless Ursula had done that.

Her soapy scent lingered, along with her musk, her taste still on his lips. A sweetly sensual flavor uniquely hers. Her curvy figure had delighted him more than he'd expected. So did her boobs crushed against his chest and her cunt snuggled to his cock. Somehow, though, her astonishing kiss beat everything else. During that small intimacy, he hadn't considered wrestling her to the floor, sucking her nipples or burying himself between her legs to sink as deep as a demon could go.

Her mouth had been enough, yet he'd also wanted more.

He was losing his mind and needed to get out of here fast. Unfortunately, Taro and Anatol kept him pinned to the wall with their dark force. No matter how hard he tried to fight them, nothing happened. "When do I get my powers back?"

"Soon as we're through." Stefin scratched his neck. "Any lingering pain in your boys?"

They hurt worse with each passing second and had plumped to the bursting point because he hadn't released their load. His rigid rod tried to point to where Ursula had last stood, his tool ready to boogie with her. "Nope."

"Are your nuts still hairy?"

"Why wouldn't they be?"

"Electrical currents, aka electrolysis, kill hair roots."

"Now you tell me? I can't move to see. Let me go so I can check."

"I'll do it." After a quick look, Anatol shook his head. "A gorilla has nothing on you. Ever hear of manscaping? MJ can probably grant you a wish and tidy you up so you don't gross out the babes. Her fees are reasonable."

"Think I'll pass." No one in this loony bin was ever touching him again, except Ursula.

He stilled, worried why he'd thought that.

Without warning, she filled his brain — melting into him, her searching gaze, a pink flush staining her cheeks, fingers slipping through his hair, keeping him to her. Like he'd be crazy enough to be anywhere else. He hadn't meant for their kiss to go so far and hadn't a clue where his passion had come from. Since his descent into Hell, he'd never been sentimental, or particularly kind, unless he wanted something, when he'd put on an act to get it.

Too easily, she'd stripped his emotions bare, taking from him while he gave.

That had to be the treatment aftereffects. These goons had drained him to the point he couldn't fight back supernaturally or emotionally.

Hill's Absinth called even louder, along with a marathon fuckfest with a dozen women. No, two dozen. Maybe more. The only way to set him on a depraved path again.

Stefin hit another key. "Done. You want a printout?"

"I'll wait for the movie."

The guys laughed and released him. Farron shook out his arms. After cracking his neck, he flung his hand and sent a fireball through this room to the next.

A female staffer dove to the floor. The zombie with her blinked dully at the smoking hole in his chest.

Stefin brought up the screen again. "You're going to have to pay for Heather to heal him and for MJ to grant our wish to fix the wall. Adding the charges to your bill."

Farron couldn't have cared less. Having his power back was like rising from the dead. Nothing could compare. Not plush lips, a clean, soapy scent or a tender, hopeful smile that made puppy dogs, kittens and baby chicks look downright cynical in comparison.

He rubbed his temples, trying to purge Ursula from his brain.

The guys filed out.

Unglued, he followed them into the hall, forgetting he could dematerialize.

Before he could flee, Becca poked his chest, stopping him. "Uh-uh. Back in the room. Now."

"No. Why? My treatment's over."

"We have to talk."

When did everyone here become so fucking chatty? "This is about Heather, right? I shouldn't have kissed her. My bad. If she needs root canals or a tongue transplant to get my taste out of her mouth, send me the bill. I'll gladly pay for it."

"Inside." She shoved him.

Arms flailing, he bumped into the table before regaining his balance. "If you're worried I kissed the guys, trust me, I didn't. If I'd had a chance, I would have vaporized them."

She slammed and locked the door. "You should have done that with yourself before kissing Ursula."

He went hotter than he usually was then cold and wondered if she could read his smutty thoughts. She was a half-witch, after all, with powers he couldn't begin to know. If not that... He lifted his face to the ceiling.

"What are you doing?"

There weren't any cameras as far as he could see. It was always possible she'd put them in the light fixture or in the aversion therapy machine. "You have me on video kissing her?"

"No. Ursula told me."

That didn't make sense. She couldn't have been upset and reported their fun. Hell, she'd come on to him. "Look, I'm no saint, but I didn't do anything wrong. We were talking, or rather I was and she was staring and — what exactly did she say happened?"

Becca gave him an exhaustive description of what he and Ursula had done, right down to their sighs and groans.

He'd lived it and hadn't recalled a tenth of those details, too caught up in the moment to notice. His cock came alive now, as it had then, and strained against his jeans. Hurt like a motherfucker but felt good too. Before Becca noticed his arousal, he folded his hands over his fly. "Oh, yeah? Is that all?"

"Try more than enough or too much. I know you're a demon, but at least have the decency to quit grinning."

He hadn't realized he was and sobered. "Is Ursula upset? Do you want me to pay for her therapy?"

"I want you to avoid her at all cost. Far be it from me to interfere in anyone's life, but she's vulnerable. She's just come off a bad romance and doesn't know what she wants. She talks big about being like Wynona without realizing exactly what that means. Nights at BDSM clubs, voyeurism, doing the nasty in ways most people haven't dreamed of. A guy like you would eat her alive, figuratively, maybe literally too. Damn you." She squeezed her fists and bounced.

"I shouldn't have kissed her, okay?"

"No, it's not. Damn you for what you're doing now."

"You mean talking to you and apologizing?"

"You're smiling again."

He strove for morbid this time and cleared his throat "So you want me to blow her off when she asks what day and time I'm picking her up for our date that she suggested. Is that it? Am I close?"

"You don't have to be cruel. Tell her you have a soul to corrupt, a possession that can't wait, rotten stuff you usually do."

His job in Hell wasn't anywhere near to what she'd described. Only the newly turned hit the bricks to recruit fresh meat. At his level, he had satisfying work he enjoyed that didn't hurt anyone. However, explaining the facts of Hell to her was useless. Like most others, she lumped demons in with bums, louses, pricks or anyone and anything that was unworthy.

Ursula's kiss said he mattered. It was nice having someone so pure honoring him for a change. It gave him hope and made him feel more like a man than sex, wealth or power could. He had to get out of here. Sadly, he couldn't budge. "What if she keeps asking?"

"She probably will. Be gentle but firm. Eventually, she'll get the hint."

"About what? That I don't want her as a woman? That I find her unattractive and would rather date a zombie than go out with her? Do you enjoy being cruel to your so-called friends?"

Becca's face turned redder than her hair. She stepped back. "I'm trying to help, not hurt her."

"Letting her make up her own mind might be the best way to do that."

"Not when it comes to you."

"Yeah, I know. I'm a pig." He shoved his hair back. "Don't worry, I hadn't planned on dating, sleeping with or even kissing her again. I know she's too good for me."

"Hey, hey, hey, I never said that. One of my best friends is a demon. I even love Taro, Stefin and Anatol when they have their heads screwed on right, which isn't often. But when it happens, they're great."

"Then Ursula's not too good for me?"

Becca spoke through her teeth. "She's not a demon. You need to stay with your own kind."

"Oh, yeah? Since when? The soul wants equality for all."

Her mouth fell open. "Where'd you hear that?"

He wasn't sure. The words had spilled from his mouth, independent from his brain. This was getting too damn weird. "I gotta go." If he had to crawl on all fours, he was taking off.

"Wait." She grabbed his arm. "Are you going to leave her alone?"

He pulled away. "I'd planned to do that before our talk. You're right. She and I don't fit. As a good angel, she'll always be out of my league. The next time I see her, I swear, I'll run in the opposite direction."

"But you'll also be nice about it, right?"

Fuck, she wanted the pissing moon. "Yeah, that, too."

He left the room and still forgot to dematerialize. That proved he'd lost the edge he'd had before coming here today. Never again would he submit to another treatment in this psycho place. If mortal babes didn't like him the way he came, too damn bad. He'd work his dark magic on them, have fun and call it a day.

Becca slapped his back.

"Hey." He glared. "That hurt. What's with everyone here?"

"Shhh." She yanked him into the room. "Ursula's rounding the corner. I don't want her to see me. Don't hurt her." She pushed him back out and skittered further inside.

Braced for whatever happened, he looked over and forgot everything Becca had said.

Chapter Four

Ursula stood at one end of the hallway, Farron at the other. They faced each other like Old West gunslingers. The battle was indeed on, though not for turf. Their feelings and future were in peril if she didn't act. However, she couldn't shake uncertainty about her new look—the perfume, her hair and dress.

Its black leather clung to her curves, leaving nothing to the imagination. Though long enough to fall mid-calf, a long slit up the left seam revealed a shocking expanse of thigh. The sweetheart neckline dipped low, its cut so tight her breasts weren't only plumped but threatened to fall out. Two meager shoulder straps held the thing up and kept her nominally decent. Long onyx-and-silver earrings dangled to her shoulders. Her platform pumps had stiletto heels embellished with black spikes.

According to Wynona, the deadly metal would keep Farron in line if he got too playful.

Ursula would have willingly gone back to her lonely nights, sans dildo or the aversion therapy machine, rather than harming him. Not only was he the hottest man she'd ever known, he looked adorable now, shell-shocked, too. His arms hung limply at his sides and his mouth sagged open.

A zombie with a hole in his chest left a treatment room, escorted by a staffer. She took one look at Farron and raced from him, yanking the client with her.

Heather met the duo halfway. "Oh, no, what happened? Never mind. Come with me. I'll make it better."

Ursula was alone with him again. He staggered toward her. She tottered to him, uncertain of her footing in the heels. To maintain balance, she had to swing her hips with each step.

He gaped. His cheeks darkened. The bulge behind his fly tented the material.

Even a good angel knew what that meant.

Her wildest hopes for them had never been this great.

His faltering steps changed to a brisk stride. Upon reaching her, he circled slowly. She turned in place, following him, eager to see his reactions no matter how dizzy the rotations made her.

"Stop." He shook his head and blinked. "Let me look at you."

Heat rushed to her throat and face.

He leaned close to her bosom, his nose almost touching the swells, and sniffed. "What is that fragrance?"

Constance had said it was amber and honey with a trace of musk. "Perfume. Don't you like it?"

"Are you kidding? Your soapy stuff was nice, but this..." His eyes flamed, casting golden lights on her chest. The spots danced. He lifted his face and took her in. "Your hair."

Her bun was history. Soft tresses fell in loose waves to her shoulders.

Farron buried his face in her do.

The best moment ever. She sagged against him.

He sniffed and growled. On a lusty groan, he pulled back. "Your face."

Liner, shadow and mascara did make one's eyes appear larger. Ursula was relatively certain hers were as rounded as his.

He stared at her mouth. Lipstick and gloss had done the trick there. His smile couldn't have been wider, his dimples deeper.

She'd wowed him.

Time to seduce. For once, that wasn't a problem, since self-assurance practically burst from her. She stroked his tattoo. His muscle jumped. She pressed her knee against his, shocked at her sudden depravity, but loving it too. "Where are you taking me? Literally and figuratively."

He pulled her closer, his bulge snuggled into her mound, giving her a taste of what would come. Warmth poured from him into her and back again. They both perspired despite the coolish night.

With his cheek pressed to hers, he settled his mouth on her ear.

Her legs went watery.

He tightened his grip, keeping her from dropping to the floor. "Everywhere I can and then some."

Her bones softened at his rich baritone. "What?"

"You asked where I'm taking you. My answer is every-fucking-where."

Heaven could never compare to this. "Okay. Will you be bold?"

He laughed. "Are you kidding? Wait till you see what's in store for —"

Loud throat clearing sounded down the hall, followed by several sharp raps.

Upon the first knock, he'd released her. The next two had him backing away.

She followed unsteadily, mostly from arousal, partly from her uncomfortable shoes. "What are you doing?"

He put additional distance between them. His bronze complexion turned a sickly gray.

"What's wrong?"

"Nothing. Stay there."

She followed. "Why? Where will you be?"

"Don't move." He grabbed her shoulders. His lids slid down and breath spilled from him. He stroked her gently, looking torn between desire and agony. "Please."

"Why?"

"Just do it." On a strangled groan, he rushed to the room where he'd been before and slipped inside.

Collapsed against the door, Farron breathed hard. Didn't help. His brain was mush, every muscle so taut the burning sting would have killed him had he been alive. If that wasn't bad enough, his balls were about to explode, his cock determined to poke a hole through his boxer briefs and jeans. In all his time in Hell, he'd never been as miserable.

Becca's glare wasn't helping. "Have you lost your ever-loving mind?" She'd spoken softly, despite her nasty question. "You were supposed to run in the opposite direction, not stick your nose in her hair."

As if he didn't already know that. She should have been on his side of the fence. One look at Ursula and he'd been a goner. One sniff and he would have done whatever she asked. He'd thought her soapy smell had been nice. Not even close. The sweet-musky scent she now wore rattled the cage Becca had put him in, while that dress... Even Ursula's skin wasn't as snug. If she made one wrong move or breathed too deeply, her nipples would pop out, the areolas possibly a delicate pink, her tips long and hard, begging for his mouth.

He shuddered and covered his junk as he had the last time.

Becca stared at his hands, his erection behind them. "What are you doing?"

Trying to deflate if she gave him a moment or two. "I need a sec." He'd spoken as quietly as she had. "Make that a few minutes."

"Time's up. You need to get out there now and tell her there isn't going to be a date. Ever. That you want her to forget you—even if Constance has to zap her memories—and that she needs to move on, preferably to one of Rafael's friends. I've seen their headshots. They're freaking hot, preppy like Eric. Go on tell her that. Not the part about the pictures or Eric, everything else. Nicely, of course."

"Yes, ma'am. And while I'm at it, I'll also establish world peace, clean the water and air, get Santa elected president and make gumdrops fall from the clouds rather than rain." He pushed away from the door. "You want me to break her damn heart?"

"She doesn't have one. She's. An. Angel. She's mostly soul."

Yeah, yeah, yeah. "You know what I mean. She went through all the trouble to get that killer dress, fix her hair and do whatever she did to her face. It looks amazing, still sweet but sexy too. Yet you actually expect me to tell her she's not going anywhere dolled up like that? Why don't I ask another woman, or a whole slew of them, to join us and I'll make out with those babes while she watches to really crush her?"

"That would be cruel."

"You should know, since your mind works that way."

"A little hurt now is better than total devastation later."

"Who says I don't agree?" He threw up his hands. "My hope is to keep her pain to a minimum. Granted, I lost my head for a moment out there. Won't happen again." He hoped. "However, that doesn't mean I'm doing things your way. She has her heart, spirit or whatever the fuck you want to call it, set on a date. I'll give her an ultra-vanilla one, behaving like the perfect gentleman. After I show her a good yet chaste time, I'll explain why we won't work out. And yeah, I'll do so nicely."

"Taking her anywhere is giving her false hope."

Him, too. But it couldn't be helped. "No matter what you say, demand or shriek, I can't let her down. Not when she's gone through so much for tonight."

Already Ursula was too precious for him to dismiss her feelings. He didn't want to imagine her disappointment or humiliation if he blew her off now. Her all dressed up with nowhere to go, no guy wanting her, not even a crappy demon. Soul-deep sorrow ached in his chest and gut. An unfamiliar emotion he didn't much like. Maybe when she was gone, he'd go back to his old ways and they wouldn't seem as empty as they were looking now. "I'd better get out there."

She grabbed his arm. "I'm sorry it has to be this way."

"Yeah, me, too." He patted her hand and forced himself not to sprint back to Ursula.

As he'd asked, she hadn't budged. Not even now when he took far too long to reach her. Something akin to tenderness washed over him, making his knees wobble.

"Are you all right? You're kind of pale." She touched his cheek.

Every nerve ending in him fired. Only a shitload of will kept him from turning his face into her palm and kissing it. Not only because he was horny but because he was touched, too, by her sweet gesture.

She regarded him. "Did you forget something?"

Only that she was too good for him. What a dumb fuck he was for not remembering that important item. "No. Why?"

"You went back to the room."

He'd already forgotten about that and Becca, though, not his promise to keep from ravishing Ursula. He'd treat her with respect tonight and leave her forever without as much as a goodbye kiss. "I went to get my smartphone." He patted his back pocket where the thing had always been. "Didn't know that's what you meant. Ready?"

She slipped her arms around his neck and rested her head on his shoulder, her boobs and pussy welded to him, her scent surrounding them. "Yes, I am. For anything."

He transported them to Paris, the Eiffel Tower specifically, though not its Jules Verne restaurant. That was for tourists. *Ce Moment dans Le Temps,* This Moment in Time, was a hangout for supernaturals, a classy place for a fine lady. Although the dining room was on the same level as Jules', this area was invisible to humans.

With the time zone difference, it was afternoon here. No biggie to change for a high-ranking demon. Farron flexed his power and turned day to night for him and Ursula alone. Thousands of stars dusted the ebony sky, adding to the magical mood. Not a wise choice, but he didn't care. This was something he had to do for her, to make tonight as special as possible because it was their only chance to be together.

His gut clenched. He ignored the pain and let wonder embrace him as it never had. Far beneath the windowed walls, the city pulsed, as alive as any creature, traffic flowing over streets like blood through veins. Twinkling lights peppered the endless view.

She turned slowly, taking everything in, lips parted, eyes sparkling, the gold in her irises far outweighing the brown.

Her delight reminded him of someone having a religious experience. Given what he was, he should have been appalled at the notion but couldn't have been more pleased.

"Wow." She touched his chest. "Thanks. This is so romantic."

Not to mention, several lightyears from being chaste, as he'd promised Becca. His boys didn't care, rippling with glee. If his cock could have offered a delighted squeal, it would have. Typical reactions for his equipment. However, he knew better than to act without concern for the future. This place and the next hour or two wouldn't change things for them. He should have brought her to Mickey D's. No one would ever accuse that place of being romantic, but she hadn't dressed for fast food. The Crucible was also out of the question. She was too good for that dive. Still, he had to make this right and keep their non-date innocent.

"You actually like this place?" He smiled wryly. "Look, we can take off, find somewhere else that rocks. You won't hurt my feelings by saying this sucks."

"Oh, no, please. I love it here." She melted into him, staring again.

Her gaze held him hostage and kept him from breathing or moving, except for his wiggling nuts and cock. She wrapped her arms around him.

He nearly exploded with desire and gratitude. Her tender caress was what every mortal or supernatural man needed—a place to come home to, banish whatever shitty stuff had happened and hunker down for pleasure that renewed hope and dreams. If he wasn't careful, he'd soon spout poetry…the sweet kind. Afraid to lose what little control he had, he didn't dare touch her in return.

"When did you change into this?" She stroked his collar. His designer silk shirt and wool slacks were blacker than the sky. "I didn't see you do so." She smiled sweetly and innocently. "I want to later when you undress. No keeping me from knowing every part of you."

She was killing him.

"Farron, my man."

Salem, a demon, friend and the maître d', offered his hand.

They shook.

"So, how's Hell?""

Farron didn't want to talk about it. "Hot."

He chuckled. "I meant your places? They doing good?"

Ursula lifted her face. "Places? Like homes? Apartments? Condos?"

Right now, he wished that were true because she hadn't come anywhere near to what he owned.

Salem barked a laugh. "Not hardly. They're—"

"Enough chitchat." Farron gripped Salem's shoulder hard enough to shatter his collarbone. "The lady's hungry. Show us to your best table."

He gagged. "Sure." Gingerly, he touched his shoulder and led them to a secluded area next to a window with an unrestricted view. No girders. A centerpiece boasting scarlet candles, red roses and baby's breath graced the white-linen tablecloth. Fine china, crystal goblets, gold utensils and a violin-piano instrumental added to the high-class milieu. Perfect for a lady like Ursula. She should never go to a place that was less.

Witches from the most respected covens dined with governing warlocks or those on the rise politically. Legendary vamps, famous weres and minor gods rounded out the crowd, everyone dressed in designer duds.

Men and women eyed Ursula. If Farron had to guess, the guys were drinking in her lush curves, the gals focusing on her dress, except for the lesbians, who probably liked both. More than a few ladies twisted in their plush velvet chairs and craned their necks to see better. Although Ursula fit right in and her looks were more outstanding than the rest, she hunched her shoulders then tugged her straps.

Now wasn't the time to bring up their doomed relationship and kill what remained of her shaky confidence. He touched her knuckles, not crazy enough to go further than that. He was only a demon, not a freaking saint. "Relax. Your dress is fine."

He spoke quietly to avoid embarrassing her.

Despite the dim lighting, her blush was obvious, her smile grateful. "Thanks. I'm glad you like it. From now on, I'll always wear dresses like this for you."

"Good evening." A waiter placed two leather-bound menus on the table. "I'm Xanther and will be your server for the meal. Back in a moment." He hurried away.

Salem trailed after him and glanced over his shoulder. "Enjoy."

Farron nodded, unable to speak. Already, Ursula had jumped past tonight to their next date and the one beyond, straight into infinity by using that six-letter word…always.

"Let me get your chair." She reached for it.

"I have it and yours." He eased her hand away and forgot to let her go.

She beamed.

This wasn't going as he'd planned. Time to get a grip. Once they both sat, he read his menu raptly, not understanding a word. Her scent made it impossible to think. More heat rushed from her than seemed feasible.

"What do you suggest we order?" She wrapped her foot around his and stroked his thumb.

His vision dimmed. "What do you like?"

"This." She kissed his fingertips.

If he'd been a girl, he would have cried. He wanted her more than reason allowed and not because she looked great. There was no defense against her sincerity and affection unless he reverted to form, fucking her because he was a depraved beast, leaving her wounded and lonely after he lost interest. He always had with other women. She'd probably be the same.

He couldn't be that callous. Savage demon or not, he'd chew off his balls before he deliberately hurt her.

He pulled his hand away. "Their baked *camembert, sole meunière, hachis parmentier* and *coquilles Saint-Jacques* are always good."

"I have no idea what that is, but I trust your judgment."

"Dammit, you shouldn't." He sure as fuck didn't.

Her smile wobbled. "What?"

"Our wine list." Xanther presented the leather-bound sheet over his forearm as knights of old had done with their swords. At least in flicks Farron had seen.

He eyed his steak knife. A jab to his carotid artery or jugular sounded nice, if could have offed himself and avoided having to deliver his 'we're through' speech to Ursula. No such luck for someone who wasn't alive. "You have Hill's Absinth, right?"

"For you, an unending amount. And what would the lady like?"

"Wait." Farron rubbed his forehead. He couldn't risk drinking and losing control. "Kill my first order. I'll have ginger ale."

"Very good. And the lady?"

"I'll try the hills stuff."

Farron laughed shrilly and sobered fast. "Not a chance. It's seventy-proof."

"Oh. What's that mean?"

Xanther leaned in. "It's strong enough to strip paint off cars and probably asphalt from roads."

She paled but pulled back her shoulders. "I'm not afraid. Bring me a bottle. No, make that two. I'm ready for anything."

"Not with that stuff you aren't. Bring her your best Chablis in a shot glass." He grabbed Xanther's bow tie and tugged him close. "Water it down before you do."

"Yes, sir. I'll take your appetizer order when I get back."

Alone with her again, Farron studied his menu like a felon preparing for an FBI grilling. The text for the *escargot, tapenade noir à la figue* and *tartare de filet de boeuf* swam before him, impossible to understand no matter how many times he read it.

She eased her foot over his ankle.

His toes curled.

"You like protecting me, don't you?"

He pulled his leg away. "Excuse me?"

"You were so masterful with the drinks, taking charge as you did and not wanting me to hurt myself. You don't know how much I appreciate your concern. I'm not used to stuff like this."

"Have you ever been on a date — that is, out with a man before?"

"Sure, with Rafael. We never went to a place like this, though. He preferred fast food or buffets, very casual, not romantic at all."

He sounded like a smart man. Farron should have asked for Rafael's guidance before embarking on this lunatic evening. Too late now, though, she had given him an opening into what he had to say. "I hear several of Rafael's friends have their eye on you."

She laughed self-consciously. "Since when? Men don't notice me. I'm invisible to them." Despite her nonchalance, hurt registered in her eyes.

He wanted to hug her from here until time ended but didn't move. "Bull. I haven't noticed you? I'm not a man?"

"Oh, no. You're more than that." She leaned against the table. "You're a demon."

Her pupils were dilated, cheeks pinked up, breasts wiggling prettily with her strained breaths. If he hadn't known better, he would have guessed she was having an orgasm. Maybe she was. This had to stop. "Other guys notice you, too." He gestured to the room.

A vamp lifted his chin in greeting to her and licked his fangs. A minor god, or a warlock, raised his champagne in acknowledgment. Two weres grinned shamelessly, one curling his forefinger, gesturing her over.

Farron bared his teeth at the prick.

"There."

"What?" He glanced at her then scanned the room.

"You gave that guy with the hairy eyebrows and thick stubble a snotty look. Protecting me again like a man, or rather a demon, should with his lady."

He cleared his throat and searched for Xanther so he had someone else to talk to. The guy was nowhere in sight. "I hear Rafael's friends are as hot as Eric. You know, the preppy look."

"No need to be jealous."

"Huh?"

"They aren't my type. I like a man who wants to kick up his heels, throw caution to the wind and will boldly go where no man has gone before."

"Like in *Star Trek*?"

"In bed." She wrapped her foot around his ankle.

He clutched the menu so tightly his thumbs dented the leather. "We have to talk."

"Okay." With one arm on the table, she leaned forward. The dress barely covered her nipples. "About what?"

He went blank, her jiggling breasts captivating him. "Ah…"

"Your drinks." Xanther placed them on the table.

She lifted her thimbleful of watered-down wine. Farron guzzled most of his ginger ale before coming up for air. He ordered duck pâté, shrimp-and-herb canapés, steak tartare and snails for appetizers.

Xanther entered the info in his Windows tablet. "You want to order the entrées now, too, along with another ginger ale?"

Farron didn't want the guy to go. That would leave him defenseless against Ursula. Cruel reality told him delay wouldn't change anything. "We'll order the entrées when you come back with our appetizers."

"You bet." He took off.

She leaned in. "What did you want to talk about?"

He avoided looking at her breasts or eyes and focused on her stroking his hand. Tingles and heat skipped up his arm. It felt so fucking wonderful he didn't want her to stop. Regrettably, there wasn't another choice. "Uh, I know you haven't dated much, except for Rafael."

"Does that bother you?"

"No." He played with her pinky. "Why should it?"

"You'll have to teach me all I don't know. Some men might not like that. It's not that I didn't want to date, but I never got the chance when I was mortal. Too dangerous. Once I was an angel, guys weren't interested in plain old frumpy me."

He should have stopped listening at the part where he'd teach her the facts of sex but hadn't. "Frumpy? Plain? Quit downing yourself. You're a beautiful woman. What do you mean too dangerous? You were mortal?"

"Oh, yeah." She lapped her wine and made a pleasured sound. "That's good. I was a Vestal Virgin."

Dumbfounded, he gawked. Only Mother Teresa would have been a worse choice for him to take on a date. "Are you serious?"

"Sure. When I was six, none of the patrician families wanted to give up their daughters to the cause, so to speak. Who could blame them? Every recruit was looking at thirty years of celibacy in the temple. You could marry after your service, but seriously, that's pretty darn late to start a family, especially during a time of endless pestilence, wars and other stuff. Most people barely lived past their teens. Vestals were supposed to be highborn, but like I said, none of them wanted to donate a kid. Although my parents were freeborn and Roman residents, they were plebes, but beggars can't be choosers so the powers-that-be took me on and away from my folks."

"When you were only six, a child?"

Tears shimmered in her eyes. Her mouth turned down. "It wasn't a nice time, but I tried to make the best of it. For the first ten years, I was a student. During the next, a servant, and finally I would have been a teacher."

"Would have been? You weren't? What happened?"

She gestured dismissively. "You don't want to hear this."

Farron pressed her hand to his chest. "I do." She looked so forlorn he not only wanted to protect her, he had to bring back her smile and naked enthusiasm. "Tell me. I won't judge."

"Thank you." She lowered her face. "When I was twenty-seven, Rome was going through some pretty bad political and economic upheavals. I didn't know anything about the events at the time or that Vestal Virgins were often used as scapegoats. A way for citizens to vent their rage at lousy taxes, failed crops, endless conflicts, whatever. You think I'm naïve about sex now. Wow, you should have seen me then."

He kissed her fingers.

A tear hung on her lashes. "I was going through my days tending the sacred fire and doing no end of boring stuff, basically admin work, when a servant or citizen — I'm still not clear on which — accused one of the other Vestals of being unchaste." She squeezed his hand. "Domitia was only sixteen and so in love. I couldn't blame her. The boy was almost prettier than she was." Ursula laughed softly. "They never did anything except stare at each other, you know?"

He did. His stomach twisted again, but he held on to her as she did him. "Go on, please."

"Gossip and especially an accusation weren't anything to ignore. The Romans took their myths seriously. I knew what was coming, so I confessed, saying that Antonius, the boy she liked, was my lover. He'd already escaped the city, which meant nothing was going to happen to him."

"What about you?"

"I couldn't let them kill Domitia."

"What? They were going to murder her for a few longing gazes?"

"Those were the rules. I knew what was coming so — "

"Wait. You said that before but didn't explain. What did they do to you?"

"Buried me alive."

"*What?*"

Several diners looked over, clacks from their utensils stopping. Even the music halted.

Ursula stroked his cheek. "It's okay. It's over. And really, it wasn't like you think. They didn't toss me in a grave or anything. They used the *Campus Sceleratus*, otherwise known as the evil field, an underground chamber. After setting up enough water and food for a few days, so I wouldn't die immediately, they filled the entrance with dirt to keep me from climbing out, even though Vestals were expected to die willingly and with dignity. Tell that to someone facing the great beyond. They did give me a chance to defend myself. Kind of rigged if you ask me. If I could have proved my chastity by carrying water in a sieve, they would have dropped the charges. Common sense tells you that wasn't going to happen with a container full of holes, so I died. But at least Domitia was all right and — "

He claimed her mouth, silencing her with his tongue, unable to hear another word. Those lousy bastards. And they called demons scum. His kind had nothing on cruel humans. He didn't want to imagine her terror, alone in a dark room with next to nothing to eat and drink, unable to get the meager rations down her throat, the crowd cheering self-righteously as she died a slow and agonizing death.

No wonder she was a good angel. She'd more than earned her white wings.

He slipped his tongue deeper, relishing her taste, needing to be close. He wanted to make her happy. If that meant a roll in the sack with him during the only date they'd share, then fucking A, he was on board. In one existence after another, everyone else had denied her.

Farron couldn't. Wouldn't. Not tonight. He pulled his mouth free. "I want to sleep with you."

Chapter Five

Everything intensified for Ursula. Colors grew brighter, sounds became more pronounced, scents richer. Musk mingled with Farron's usual fragrance, creating an irresistible combination that made her head swim.

He wanted her.

She'd waited a lifetime then an eternity for a man to declare himself with such passion. Although giddy with boundless hope, she still needed clarification. "You do mean sex, right? Not just us snoozing together in the same bed?"

His explosive laughter was joyous not unkind. Affection blazed in his eyes. "Yeah, I mean sex. The excitement you've missed and want to experience. The whole enchilada."

He kissed her again, more forcefully than before but with genuine tenderness. A miracle, especially since he'd tried to put distance between them scant minutes before.

Thank goodness, Constance had prepared Ursula for his behavior. She pulled her aside while the others had argued over dresses, lingerie and shoes during the makeover. Ursula had expected to get a lecture for liking him.

What happened wasn't close.

Constance hugged her. "Don't you worry what anyone thinks about you and Farron liking each other. I know we gave you a hard time before, but that's not going to happen again, as far as I'm concerned. This is your thing, not anyone else's. Go for what you want with everything you have."

Terror struck her. "That's not much."

"Bull. I don't want to hear that defeatist shit from you again. And don't let him put you off if he tries."

That didn't sound good. "What do you mean? This is a date, so it has to be good, right?"

"Not always."

She got nauseated. "How would he put me off?"

"By playing down your time together, pretending you're only friends and mentioning other guys you might like. If he does that or anything close to it, play dumb. Keep your focus on him. Bring that demon to his knees. Seduce the fuck out of him."

He dove in for another kiss, his tongue filling her mouth, his thumb caressing her cheek.

She cupped his.

When he'd tried to push her onto Rafael's friends, she'd done as Constance had advised and pretended she didn't know what he was doing. No one had to tell her Becca was behind his words. He'd spent enough time in the treatment room with her, claiming to be retrieving his phone.

Didn't matter what he'd planned to do on her orders, Ursula had him now. She hoped.

Another thought intruded, ruining the moment. She eased her mouth from his.

He rested his forehead against hers and panted like a whipped dog.

She loved her effect on him but her stomach still clenched at what she had to ask. If she could have avoided the subject, she would have, but needed to know the truth more. "What I told you about my past..." She hadn't intended to mention those times to him. The words simply slipped out. "You're not feeling sorry for me because of that, are you?"

She hoped that wasn't why he wanted her again.

He pulled back and stared. No, he glowered. "You mean pity?"

"That, too."

He made a nasty face, truly demonic, then huffed. "I'm insulted you asked. You're the bravest woman I've ever known. You should be pitying me and everyone else in this damn place because we're not as a good as—"

"No, don't say that, ever. You're amazing." She sprinkled him with kisses to keep him from arguing and didn't stop until he heaved air again. "Let's go. Wait. Where are we going? I'd love to take you to my place, but security's unbelievably tight in Heaven. What about your places? I don't care if they're not an apartment, house or condo. A tent will work. Outside's good too. Or we can use a treatment room at the service or—"

He pressed his finger to her mouth. "Let me take care of where we'll be going later. All right?"

No, it wasn't. She'd expected them to leave immediately, not later. In her world, that didn't sound good because the delay would give him a chance to change his mind again. Second time tonight, particularly if Becca called and laid down the law.

Recalling Constance's sage advice, Ursula drew his finger between her lips and sucked playfully.

He grinned. His eye flames bobbed like nobody's business.

She had him now. "Why not right away?"

"Why not right away what?"

She eased his finger from her mouth. "Us leaving here? We can have the kitchen put our food in a doggie bag. If you're worried about hurting Xanther's feelings because we're taking off, I'll promise him a big tip. I'm good for it."

"You'll do no such thing. Tonight's on me. And we're eating here."

"Why? I'm hungry for you, not food." She cradled his hand to her breasts.

Color shot to his cheeks. His flames gave off more light than the flickering candles. "Ah…"

"Yes?" She huddled closer.

He stroked her mounds.

They tingled. "More."

"More what?"

"Touching me where you are."

He lowered his head, shook it and pulled back his hands. "Later."

"Why not now?"

"Hold it for one sec." He inhaled deeply. "Before we go through that verbal dance again, we *will* boogie the night away. I swear. But before we do that, there will be this." He gestured to the restaurant. "You've never had a real date. The kind you'll never forget. I want to give that to you. I don't want to rush this."

She threw her arms around him, overwhelmed with too many emotions — surprise, pleasure, gratitude and love. Admittedly, she was insane to fall this fast for anyone, even a hunk like Farron, but she couldn't help herself. No man had ever treated her as he did. Rafael had been kind and considerate, but stingy with his affection. She'd been starved for that more than anything else and had willingly accepted so little to ease her gnawing loneliness. "Yes, of course we'll have a real date. No rushing, only enjoying."

A bus boy arrived, filled their water glasses and delivered a baguette, creamy butter and a cheese plate. On his heels, Xanther approached. His huge tray held several platters. Steam rose from the first he set down. Snails.

Ursula suppressed a shudder. The last time she'd seen those things was in the temple gardens before she'd died.

"Why the face?" Farron speared a critter then dipped it into a tiny container filled with bubbling yellow sauce. "You've never tried these?"

"They're not on Mickey D's or HomeTown Buffet's menus."

He laughed.

Xanther set the last plate down, along with another ginger ale. "Do you need a few minutes to decide on your entrées?"

"Nope. We'll have *soupe à l'oignon, sole meunière, hachis parmentier* and for dessert *Mont Blanc*." Farron winked at her. "Sound good?"

She hadn't understood most of what he'd said but loved how he sounded. No wonder they called French a romance language. "Marvelous."

"Shoo." He gestured Xanther away. "The lady and I want to be alone."

She shivered with anticipation.

He slipped his hand beneath her chin and brought the snail to her mouth. "Open up, no arguments. There isn't any reason to be afraid. These won't bite. They're dead."

That didn't stimulate her appetite, though, his touch was phenomenal. She parted her lips willingly. First to the food. Later, she'd do the same to every blessed part of him, even his gorgeous toes.

He stroked her throat. "Good?"

Her thoughts were beyond decadent and starred them rolling across a bed, grass or possibly water. Wherever he wanted to take her. Of course, he was asking about the food. The meat was surprisingly buttery, the flavoring light, just a trace of garlic and onion. "Yeah. You know so much. Do you come here often?"

"Couple of times a year." He cut a small piece from a whitish square veined with cream and brown then speared the morsel. "Try this."

"What is it?"

"Duck pate."

The delightfully smooth texture tasted like ginger, nutmeg and nuts enhanced by bacon. "Wow, that's good."

He offered the steak tartare next.

She leaned away. "Sorry, I don't do raw meat."

"Later you will."

To her surprise, she laughed and blushed equally, her fevered state caused by elation not shame. "Here, let me." She scooped tartare onto a fork and brought the sorry mess to his lips.

He sucked her thumb then accepted the offering, his gaze on her.

She fell more in love with him for his priceless attention. "Tell me about you. Everything."

His chews slowed. Caution filled his beautiful face.

She'd crossed the line, uncertain whether he didn't want to share because he had no intention of going deeper than friendship or because he was ashamed of what he'd done in the past. "Please, tell me. I won't judge."

He hadn't done so with her. His encouragement had meant more than he could have imagined.

"Not much to tell." He bit into a light-pink canapé with a single shrimp and scallion on top.

"Who were you when you were mortal? Where did you grow up? What was your family like? What happened to send you to...uh..."

"Hell, Hades, the Great Inferno, No Man's Land?"

Ashamed for asking such a rude question, she hung her head. "I shouldn't have pried. Whatever happened, I'm sure you had a good reason for what you did."

"Are you going to cry?"

She might if she'd hurt him badly. "Are you?"

He lifted her chin. "Guys don't do that, especially demons."

"I don't care why you are one. I know you're a good man."

"You don't know me at all."

"I've seen how you've been with me. Unless… You're not trying to seduce me, are you?"

He wrinkled his nose. "You think I'd screw around with your feelings to get what I wanted?"

"Isn't that what guys do?"

He grew thoughtful and nodded. "True, but I'm not playing with you. At least not yet."

She slapped his hand from her bosom, kissed the part she'd struck then pressed his palm to her right breast. Indecent, she knew, but the other diners were exchanging tongues. More than one lady sat on her date's lap. Even the music added to the sensual scene, the deep-throated sax mingling with a sexy double bass. "Be serious."

"I thought this date was about fun."

The best enjoyment would be them getting to know each other. Since she was reluctant to reveal too much of her hope for their future, she fed him a pale-green canapé that had a radish slice and olive on top. "I'm having a great time."

He swiped his napkin across his lips. "Just a suggestion, but you need to work on your poker face. You look disappointed, not ecstatic. Maybe I can help. I've never been mortal. From what you've told me about your life, I'm glad I missed out on the being born and dying thing. Especially the last part. Sounds like it sucks."

It had. She pushed those awful memories away. "Are you actually a fallen angel?"

He threw out his arms. "That's me."

Wow. She'd never met an FA. "You're real close to Satan, huh?"

"Related. First cousins, actually."

"No fooling?" She accepted the tartare from him without realizing what she was doing, made a face then blinked at the rich, salty flavor. "This is good."

"I know."

She chewed and swallowed quickly. "Do you mind me asking what happened during the big battle upstairs? New arrivals in Heaven study the history, of course, but I'd like to hear your side as to why you and the others were kicked out."

"What did your history course say?"

Nothing nice. Not that she could tell him anything hurtful, nor could she lie. That only left sugarcoating the truth. "Pride got in Satan's way because he wanted to run things. It was either his way or else, no discussion or compromise. I'm not being critical when I say this, but his reasoning is like Becca hiring Taro as an enforcer then he turns and tells her it's his business now. That doesn't sound fair or right."

"Point taken. But what about new blood coming in and shaking up the status quo to make things even better? To hear S talk, he wasn't trying to overthrow anyone. He simply wanted elections, like mortals eventually had. Let the angels decide who they wanted as a leader and where the group was going. Granted, he can be a mean SOB at times — we've butted heads more than once — but he has his reasons, considering he used to live on high. That's a lot to have snatched away. No matter what he's done, he isn't as bad as mortals or your history course makes out. He simply challenged authority, like everyone else does from time to time, and that led to his downfall."

"What about yours?"

"As they say, blood is thicker than water. He talked a good game. Had me and our other cousins all riled up to get out the vote for him. When he got tossed from on high, we felt bad and followed him straight down to where he is now. Honestly, I didn't think the feud would last as long as it has. Both he and the Big Guy are stubborn dudes."

"Do you regret what you did? Is Hell as awful as I've heard?"

"Depends. What did you hear?"

"Newly dead mortals and those who cause trouble down there have to bathe in burning sulfur pits and swallow hot tar rather than water when they're thirsty. Those who complain about that have their limbs torn off and stuck back on only to go through the process endlessly. No matter how painful the torture is, shrieking isn't allowed. The condemned have to be — are you laughing at me?"

He held up his hand. "Sorry. Give me a sec." Took him several to sober. "Remember when you said Heaven has tight security? You think Hell's any different? Those urban myths about it being a shithole keep undesirables away. Mainly conservatives, fanatics and self-righteous turds who'd die if they cracked a smile and don't want anyone else having a good time, either. What maniac decided sex was bad? What idiot ruled that you couldn't eat and drink to your heart's content? Sure, it's bad for mortals' health if they overdo, but we're not human, so what's the harm?" He pushed his hair back. "No matter the bad rap Hell gets, it's worked in our favor. We don't need body scanners or eye-recognition systems to keep jerks out. We've managed that because our reputation precedes us."

She gobbled the remaining tartare. "Then it's nice down there?"

"I didn't say that. It has a lot of freedom you don't get in Heaven, along with heat, smoke and a sulfur stink, like me."

"What? Oh, no, you smell awesome." She buried her face in his neck and inhaled deeply. His cologne was masculine and rich, enhanced by the sulfur and his natural musk.

He quivered. "You mean that?"

"Absolutely." She sucked his throat.

He groaned savagely.

Pleased at his response, she indulged a little more then eased back. "Do you ever miss fresh air, the sky, clouds?"

"When I do, I come to the surface. Actually, I have the best of both worlds."

She believed him and hugged his arm, excited about the sudden possibilities for their future. Since he wasn't stuck in Hell on a permanent basis, they could find a place on Earth where they could live.

"Hope you guys are hungry." Xanther placed his tray on a stand and gestured to the sizzling dishes. "Who gets what?"

She pressed her cheek to Farron's bicep. "We'll share, both of us getting the best of whatever there is."

He shouldn't have painted such a rosy picture of Hell. It wasn't the worst spot in the universe but no sane person would consider it Disneyland, either. Except Ursula. She wore a dreamy look.

One glance at how his digs really looked, rather than the illusion he created, would wipe the gentle smile from her face. Pure horror would replace it. And his places were damn nice. S reserved the truly toxic dumps for serial killers, politicians, hedge fund managers and reality show stars. Those jerks were pure evil, polluting everything they touched. Thankfully, they didn't roam freely as he and other demons did.

Especially him. Being an FA and S's cousin gave him tons more independence and privilege than an ordinary schmo.

"Tell me about your places down there."

He forced a smile. "You mean between my legs?"

Her face flamed. "No. That is, I do want to hear about and see your, uh, stuff, but I was speaking of Hell."

She couldn't want to visit there. "Why?"

She tasted the *soupe à l'oignon* and sighed breathily. "This is amazing. You have to try it." She eased the thick onion soup, which was more bread pudding than anything, into his mouth. "Good?"

Her stroking his throat certainly was. He swallowed without chewing as Daemon always did. "Great."

"Tell me. I want to know." She circled his top shirt button and dipped lower to his belly. There, she traced his navel.

His cock shot halfway down his thigh, lengthening more than it should have. Before she pushed him into climax and the mess that would create in his pants, he rested his hand on hers. "You look hungry."

"I am. For information."

He was hoping for food. Unwilling to debate the matter, he gave her a heaping forkful of *hachis parmentier*, juicy ground beef layered with cheesy mashed potatoes.

She moaned like a woman having a kick-ass climax.

Pleased, he slipped a slice of *sole meunière* between his lips and offered her the other end.

She devoured the fish as quickly as he did, their mouths touching. Her tongue filled him, her unique flavor better than any food. They ignored their utensils and fed each other mouth-to mouth. By the time

Xanther had cleared the plates and delivered the *Mont Blanc*, Ursula was on Farron's lap.

She stroked his collarbone.

His rod pressed into her meaty ass. "Ready for dessert?"

"That and more."

Chuckling, he fed her a small bite of the chestnut crème and meringue cake. She licked powdered sugar off his fingers. They stared again then necked, tasting each other, swaying in time to the haunting music, a slow and seductive tune.

He pulled free, barely able to catch his breath. "Enough of this." With her in his arms, he stood and carried her to the small dance floor.

She regarded the couples clinging to each other. Many made lewd sounds. "You want to dance?"

He needed to give her the night of her life, to make up for the bad she'd known, and didn't want to consider what would happen after these moments ended. Certainly not her visiting Hell or having a repeat date with him. He wasn't that strong or lucky. There was no place in Heaven for an FA and she was simply too wonderful to stick one toe in his world. "Yeah, I do want to dance, but only with you."

He put her down and stroked her silky back. Her dress dipped low on her buttocks and revealed an amazing expanse of skin.

She shivered.

"Am I rubbing too hard?"

"No. Feels good." She trembled.

"Are you cold…or afraid to dance?"

She hid her face in his shoulder. "Embarrassed. I don't know how."

"I'll teach you." That's what he'd promised to do, or had he? Farron couldn't recall who'd come up with that plan. Maybe they both had. "Follow me."

Clomping along, she stepped on his foot repeatedly and jumped away.

He gathered her right back into him.

She whimpered. "I'm horrible at this. Did I break your toe the last time?"

"Nope. Barely felt it." She could have set his hair on fire and he wouldn't have noticed anything except his aching rod nestled against her sweet cunt. Eternal damnation and oppressive heat had nothing on the pain he experienced now, being so close yet still so far. Pulling himself together, he cuddled her and encouraged her to do the same with him. "Relax. Enjoy."

At last she did and swayed with him to the music. Showing off, he dipped her. She squealed happily. A miraculous sound that reached his darkest depths and delivered yearning so deep he couldn't push it away. They laughed and kissed, spinning faster and faster beneath his power until the world had blurred.

He finally slowed and smiled.

She gaped at the *Arc de Triomphe,* lit only for her, with them on top. Wind tugged their hair and clothes. She clutched him.

"No reason to be scared. I have you." He tightened his arm around her waist. An unnecessary measure. If she fell, she had wings to help her float gently to the ground. Farron was glad she hadn't used them. Protecting her was nice. Something he'd never done for another person. Funny thing, until she came along, safeguarding someone hadn't crossed his mind.

She peered down. "Can the people see us?"

"No. Do you want them to?"

"Better not. Don't want anyone having an accident. This is amazing."

"You haven't seen anything yet." For some reason, he needed to impress her, the same as human men did with their dates. Whether they were mortal or supernatural, guys were so juvenile. A matter S probably would have made worse if he'd gotten the throne upstairs. "Hang on."

He spun them away.

She yelped but giggled, too. "Where are we going?"

They stopped on the Seine riverbank, the night still an illusion he'd created for her. The same as the cruise ship decorated with white lights. Laughing and dining patrons filled the interior. The people looked real but didn't exist.

She pointed at the boat. "I love that. Let's take it next time. Okay?"

His stupid grin faded at her hope for the future. Before she noticed his dismay, he pointed up. "Look."

Red, yellow, purple and green fireworks burst overhead. Water reflected the sparkling explosions. Another illusion, no different from their time together.

Awe filled her eyes. "Are there fireworks here every night?"

He could lie, but didn't want to. Not to her. "I did those for you."

She hugged him. "Can anyone see us here?"

"Not unless you want them to."

"I don't." She cupped his ass and shoved her tongue in his mouth.

Every doubt he had about their nonexistent prospects evaporated with her incredible softness and heat. He pulled her closer, sucked her deeper, no longer willing to wait for intimacy. She was ready. He'd passed that point hours ago.

Air snapped around them, electricity flashed, his speed great enough to break the light and sound barriers. The world boomed in protest.

Then everything quieted.

Ursula pulled her hair off her face and smoothed his. "Where are—"

She stilled then slipped from his embrace and took in the wrought-iron staircase, priceless oils in gilded frames, vintage furniture upholstered in satin and velvet, potted plants, candelabras with red candles and sparkling crystal chandeliers as large as industrial-size refrigerators.

After exploring down here, she raced up the stairs. He followed slowly, giving her time to drink everything in. Her heels clicked to the right then hurried to the left. He found her in the master suite, its beveled ceiling thirty feet high and decorated with two chandeliers that dwarfed the ones on the first floor.

She touched the lacy white comforter on the cherry-wood bed, a king-size canopy model. Delicate fabric cascaded down each post. Countless roses scented the yawning room. She turned to him. "What is this place?"

"A villa."

"Yours?"

He smiled. "No. Don't worry, though. It's empty."

"Why?"

"The banker who owns it hasn't found a buyer yet."

"Where is it—that is, where are we?"

He gestured to the tall window draped in red velvet and sheer white panels.

She shoved them aside and stilled at the Colosseum in the distance, lit as it would be at night. "You brought me to Rome?"

"What happened to you in this city shouldn't have. I want your next memories of this place to be far better." He hoped she'd have a chance to embrace her sexuality during these hours and realize she was the most dazzling creature in the universe. She deserved happiness and love from a man worthy of her.

Not him. Never him. However, he'd set her on the course to her real future.

In a flash, his clothes disappeared. Naked, unashamed and fully aroused, he padded to her.

Chapter Six

Ursula dropped her hand from the curtain.

Each step Farron took caused lights to blink on one by one. It was as if the chandeliers were living things awakening after slumber. In quick succession, they blazed. The wall fixtures also flickered to life, adding to the brightness. Long red candles in ornate stands came on next. The wicks sputtered then flared, the flames nowhere near as strong as the ones in his eyes.

She gripped the drape to keep on her feet.

Smiling wolfishly, he stalked to her with a panther's grace, muscles rippling in his powerful calves and thighs, biceps flexing. His tattoo danced, the design a series of brutal black lines swirled to resemble fire. Licking them would be a gift. His impossibly broad shoulders were breathtaking.

Her mouth went dry.

His chest was nothing but hard muscle beneath smooth bronze skin, his tiny nipples reddish-brown, resembling mahogany, the halos constricted, tips erect.

No man, angel or demon could have had more perfect pecs and abs. They appeared sculpted, too defined to be real. Short, dark hairs spiraled around his navel and trailed in a thin line to his uh, his uh...

Every lewd word used to describe a man's equipment bombarded Ursula. She'd heard them all and repeatedly from Wynona and Constance when they chatted about their respective guys. No term seemed adequate to describe Farron's stuff.

It was simply glorious, his male member impossibly hard. The turgid crown defied gravity to point at her, his shaft thick and virile. Prominent veins graced the rigid column, its root nested in dense black curls. Their musky fragrance filled the suite. His weighty sac was tight to his body, the ruddy skin furred with short, dark hairs, the same as his legs and forearms.

The room whirled. She locked her knees. Her mouth moved but no words sounded.

He stopped short, concern on his face. "There's no reason to be afraid."

"I-I-I—"

"Relax. Everything's okay. I won't hurt you."

She gripped his arms.

He cradled her elbows. "You all right?"

More like stunned, aroused and thrilled. Also, angry at existence and herself. She'd spent millennia without moments like these, which left her alone, yearning and always trying to do the right thing. How wrong she'd been to deprive herself. The ladies at the service had the right idea—go for it with both arms held wide open. Hers were too weak to lift any higher. "You're so beautiful. I've never seen—I didn't think it was possible for—you're prettier than me."

That was saying something, since she looked good tonight.

He frowned. "Bull. You're exquisite."

"Not like you."

"Seriously?"

His uncertainty surprised her. "Haven't you ever looked in a mirror? If I had your gifts, I'd be like Narcissus in Greek mythology and would never stop admiring myself until I wasted away." Ogling Farron like that would be easy.

He flushed. "Looks like you've read too many myths. I'll bet you're totally into romances, too."

Only the sweet ones for their emotional punch. She sensed that was going to change after whatever happened tonight. "At first I thought you resembled a cover model but I was wrong. You're way better than those guys."

His cheeks and forehead turned red. "I'm okay as men go. You don't think I'm too hairy?"

Dark, silky strands peeked from his pits, as they should on a man. Stubble shadowed his cheeks, chin and upper lip, exactly as every female wet dream required. "I'm not following. Too hairy where?"

"My nuts."

The crude term made her blush worse than he did. What a pair they made. Perfect for each other, exactly as she'd predicted. Although she tried, she couldn't focus on anything except his plump, uh, plump... She couldn't even think the word. Didn't matter. Those babies were beefier than earlier, the perfect size and shape for her palm. She cupped them and nearly died. Hot didn't begin to describe their searing heat, though they didn't burn. The hair-roughened skin called to everything wanton within her, the weight enchanting.

"They're perfect." If she'd had a pair, she would have played with them non-stop. "Why would you think otherwise?"

He pressed into her touch, his breath strained, cheeks darkening further. "Anatol said I looked like a gorilla. He suggested manscaping."

"What's that?"

"MJ tidying me up for a reasonable fee."

Jealousy surged through Ursula so quickly, she gripped his sac to maintain control.

He yelped.

"Sorry." She loosened her hold and took care fondling him. "You okay?"

His eyes had rolled up, showing the whites. He gulped air, his color going from deep maroon to a more reasonable beat red. "Yeah."

"You're not going to let MJ do anything to your, uh…" She cleared the catch in her throat. "You're not, are you?"

"Fuck no. What Anatol and the others did was enough."

"They touched you down there? Why would they be messing with your, uh…"

"Balls. Go on. Use the word. You won't be struck dead by a bolt from above."

Easy for him to say. During her time on Earth, any unchaste thought would have had the citizens gearing up for their fave entertainment—a Vestal Virgin's execution. Fat lot of good her G-rated mind and behavior had done for her in the end, though, she still didn't mind having helped Domitia. Hopefully, she'd hooked up with Antonius and they hadn't given their female children to the cause. As far as Heaven was concerned, the uber security there wasn't only to keep undesirables out but to make sure the residents didn't deviate from form. "This is who I am."

"I beg to differ. You were taught to be meek and pure." He cradled her hand that cupped his sac and squeezed gently. "This is who you truly are. A few seconds ago, you did what comes naturally without any urging from me. I want you to give in to your naughty side now and say the word. No, fuck that. Say them all. We're not budging from this spot until you do."

That could take their entire existence. Not minding in the least, she stayed mute.

He cupped her breast. It popped out of her dress. Grinning broadly, he tested its weight and thumbed her nipple.

Delight bubbled up better than it did after she tasted chocolate, took a cool bath on a sticky day or cuddled with a kitten. Warmth, excitement and outrageous tingling coursed from her areola to her throat and belly. She pushed into him, wanting more. No, she demanded satisfaction.

He arched one dark eyebrow and stopped.

Wynona would have called him an SOB for doing so. Ursula had never known any man as hot and couldn't deny him or herself any longer. "Bah, bah, bah…"

Darn. The word wouldn't come out.

Confusion swept his face. "Is that good angel speak? If so, it's a dialect I've never heard. Can you translate?"

A cook could have fried an egg on her face. "I'm trying to do what you asked."

"Ah. Have at it." He waited, not helping.

Determined, she squared her shoulders. "Bahhhhlls." Whipped, she slumped.

"Is that a word?" He searched her face. "Or are you about to be sick? Maybe cry?"

She wanted to kick him for teasing at a time like this but fondled his genitals instead. His breath whooshed out. So did hers. "Balls."

He thumbed her nipple once then played dead again.

She sneered and let loose. "Nuts, cock, rod, shaft, boys, testicles, gonads, scrotum, plums, seeds —"

"Whoa. You lost me on the last few, but the first were great. Didn't know you were so knowledgeable."

"I'm not." She shrugged. "Constance, Wynona and MJ talk. I listen." She'd done other things, too, which she wasn't going to get into now.

Farron looked intrigued. "You listen? I believe the word you mean is eavesdrop. Not that I'm complaining." He flashed a grin then affected his stern look again.

It made him even hotter. Like a Dom. She knew about some of that stuff, too. "Me either."

"Glad we're on the same page. Now, what about those terms that describe you?"

At last, he'd asked for something easy. "Inhibited, conservative, frumpy, dull, uninterest —"

"Hold it. Are you going to make me spank you?"

She broke out in a cold sweat that did nothing to cool her sizzling skin. "What?"

"Didn't I warn you not to down yourself?" He turned her to the side, swatted her butt then pulled her back to face him. "Go on. Say the words that describe your sexiest parts. Preferably the ones Wynona, MJ and Constance use."

The ache between her legs didn't allow her to speak immediately. Moisture dampened her folds. A pulse ticked deep inside. "Uh, pussy…boobs…sheath…cleft, channel, slit, clit, kernel, nub, ass, hot, hard, wet, drenched, tight, slick, wow."

He searched her face. "How do you feel?"

Drained yet exhilarated. "Great." She bounced in delight. "They're just words."

"That's all. Nothing to be afraid of, baby."

She stilled at his endearment, tears filling her eyes. Before he noticed, she blinked them away, afraid to show too much emotion and scare him off. Whenever she got sentimental with Rafael, he hadn't been able to wing away fast enough.

Farron stroked her nipple, making it so tight, her skin stung.

She welcomed the pain, as delicious as the tension between her legs. Or rather, her pussy. She was his woman from here on out and should behave like it. "What now?"

He lifted his face, his gaze distracted. "Huh?"

"What do we do now?"

He latched on to her breast and sucked her nipple, his passion pure man. Nothing on Earth, Heaven or in the universe could match such heat and pleasure. Dazed, she gripped his head and worked his boys, running her thumbnail over the wrinkly skin. It rippled.

He shuddered and released her, his eyes wild. "Not enough. Ditch the dress. Leave the shoes on, they're epic." His grin spread from ear to ear.

She adored his enthusiasm, but the glowing chandeliers and open drapes gave her pause. Even if the sun had shone directly inside, the room couldn't have been brighter, nor could they have been more exposed to passersby. "What about the lights?"

"Right, I forgot."

A spotlight materialized. On a metallic click, its light shone on her, the beam so bright her dress had turned gray and her eyes ached. She squinted. "I meant, turn them off. Kill the wall fixtures and candles, too."

He threw back his head and laughed. "No way." He lowered his face and sobered. "I want to see every part of you."

She'd been afraid of that. "What about the people outside?"

"I'm not interested in them. Only you."

Her dress disappeared. She gasped.

He leered at her black satin-and-lace bra, a model made for a dress without a back and low-cut top. The half-cups exposed her nipples, both constricted, one damp from his mouth. He prowled lower to the scrap that made up her thong, the silk so sheer her curls peeked through. "Sweet."

The lingerie evaporated, leaving her nude except for her heels and earrings. She shook so badly, the metal jangled.

His smirk faded. "Why so scared?"

"The people." With one hand covering her ass, she jabbed her thumb at the window behind her.

"They can't see in here." He leaned in. "Ever think how hot it would be if they could and watched us?"

His file had said he enjoyed voyeurism. She didn't want to deny him, but… "It may take me a few secs to get used to that."

"No prob. Right now is for you and me. Let me look at you."

Faster than a blink, she stood on a pedestal that appeared from nowhere, except in his racy thoughts.

She staggered and flung her arms out to steady herself. Wasn't easy. The platform hovered above the floor, too far for her to jump off, unless she wanted to sprain an ankle or worse. Of course, she could always use her wings.

Despite her vigorous straining, they wouldn't unfurl. "Are you doing that?"

"Doing what?"

The spotlight clicked up several notches. Its blinding light shone directly on her. With his hands clasped in back, Farron circled at an exceedingly slow pace and took her in as Roman masters had when they'd purchased slaves.

Her pussy got even damper, arousal battling with her normal reserve. Unfortunately, insecurity won. She pressed her thighs together and tottered in a tight circle, following him.

"Do you want another spanking?"

She did, having enjoyed his playful swat. "Maybe."

He worked his mouth, trying hard not to smile. "If you keep moving, you won't get one."

What a louse. Like the other bad words she knew, she'd learned that one from the ladies...and other places. She stopped turning.

"Put your arms to the side, palms up."

Ursula hunched even more. "No need to worry about me, I'm comfortable like this." She'd draped one arm across her breasts, her free hand over her delicate curls, knees and thighs welded together.

A hurricane-force wind slammed into her. Startled, she threw out her arms and spread her legs to keep from falling.

"Nice. Keep that pose." He stepped back. "And play with yourself."

"What?"

"I forgot. You don't know how. I'll show you."

An invisible force plucked her nipples. Fingers she couldn't see stroked her clit. Something else held her tight, keeping her from curling into a fetal position.

He looked up. "Chill. It's just foreplay, nothing to worry about."

Wrong. It was a big deal. No man had ever wanted to play with her as Farron did. The sex she'd experienced was supposed to relieve tension, nothing more, but left a bigger void within. The emptiness so deep it seemed impossible to fill.

This was different.

Her shoulders relaxed first. Warmth seeped from her boobs to her belly, reached her cleft and travelled down her legs. She dug her toes into her high heels to keep upright.

Beneath the unseen force, her clit thrummed, her folds beyond damp, legs rubbery. A firm yet frisky tug on her nipple pulled a breathy gasp from her. She wanted more. With her head lolled back, she pressed into the intangible hand that was no longer there. She was the one rolling her nipples between her fingers and working her nub.

What might have embarrassed her a moment before didn't now. She played with herself as Farron had wanted, but refused to reach climax despite the coiling tension between her legs. Her pleasure belonged to them both. Panting, she lowered her face.

He breathed as hard as she did, sin in his eyes. "Don't stop."

"I won't when your hands are on me." She jumped into his arms, gripped his shoulders and wrapped her legs around his waist.

He stumbled back at her weight, but righted himself quickly and devoured her mouth as she did his. Their sloppy kiss knew no end. She groped his ass. He did the same with her boobs and torso. They clung to each other like Leonardo and Kate had as the Titanic sank.

Farron lurched to the bed and dropped them on the mattress. The frame rattled. Springs pinged. They rolled to the right, left and back, identical to her smutty fantasies. At last, he used his superior weight and size to pin her down.

She wasn't about to complain.

Locks dangled over his forehead. His chest heaved with his rough breaths and his cock settled nicely and snugly against her slit. He flexed his rod.

She cupped his face and sucked his throat hard.

Farron squirmed. "What are you doing?"

What a woman in lust has to…she was leaving her mark so no other female would dare approach him. Wynona had told Constance that she'd branded Rafael with her mouth after he'd begged her to corrupt him. Complying, she'd given him the mother of all hickeys, claiming him for her own.

"That stings. Ouch." He pushed up. His shoulder hit her nose. "Oh, shit, I'm sorry. Are you okay?"

"Fine." She rubbed her face against his shoulder. "Doesn't hurt at all. Mount me. Fill me. Make me a woman. Claim what's yours."

His chuckle pushed his belly into hers. "Someone's been reading racy novels."

The truly X-rated ones had been included in her treatment plan. Ursula had consumed the paperbacks eagerly, alternately snickering and drooling at what the heroes did with their ladies, though she still liked the sentimental scenes in the sweet romances the best. "I'm being too corny again, aren't I? Sorry. Let's try this —

screw me blind, fuck me raw, turn me every which way but loose."

"How about I pleasure you?"

"You already are." His big body was a balm she hadn't believed existed, his strength and warmth filling the desolation inside. "But, if you want to do more, I won't stop you."

"Thanks, I appreciate it."

He was having fun, not making it at her expense. For that alone, she loved him even more. He held her hands to each side and sucked her nipples, giving each their due. Her skin was super sensitive to his licks. Heat flowed from her breasts and pooled in her groin. Her channel was congested, hungry for his rod.

If Farron noticed, he didn't use the moment to mount her.

She hoped he would, eventually. Surely, that was on tonight's menu.

After stroking her juicy cleft, he made a contented sound and ran his thumb over her clit.

She bucked from surprise and a feeling that dashed through her like lightning. A hitherto unknown delight in her previously barren existence, as far as foreplay was concerned.

Holding her down with his strength, he claimed her mouth. Even if she could have managed a sound, his tongue would have muted it. This was legendary. Beyond anything she'd ever expected.

He slipped a finger into her sheath. Another followed, filling and stretching her.

Trapped, she surrendered even more, her kiss eager, her flesh his.

Their scents blended, creating a fragrance that spoke of lust, desire, tenderness and love. This had to be the beginning of their future. She'd accept nothing less.

His impassioned attention said she mattered. No one had ever treated her like this. She'd always been someone who was simply available for use as a handmaid during her Vestal Virgin days, or as an on-and-off lover for Rafael. In both instances, the men in her world had forgotten her quickly. Not Farron. He worked at pleasuring her, rubbing her clit fast, slow, hard and soft, giving her no chance for control or to know what he'd do next.

She writhed beneath him, though, not to get away — to reach climax and relieve the stunning pressure between her legs. A few more strokes were all she needed.

He pulled his mouth free and his hand away then slid down her.

Panicked, Ursula grabbed his hair before he got too far. "Where are you going?" She swallowed hard and panted. "I'm not through."

Laughing, he loosened her grip. "Neither am I."

Settled between her legs, he separated her folds. The spotlight swung to her cleft and shone even brighter, heating her skin.

She fell back, torn between groaning and giggling. This exceeded the raunchy erotica she'd read.

"Doing okay?"

She never wanted this to end. "I'm ready for anything."

"Good to hear." He spread her wide, rested her calves on his shoulders and pressed his face to her cleft.

Someone squealed. Might have been her, she wasn't sure. Sounds drifted away. Within the mega-strong light, colors faded. Her world shrank to Farron slipping two fingers back inside her channel. Once he'd imprisoned her, he licked her nub.

She stiffened, too much pleasure overpowering her.

He stroked her anus. The taut ring constricted instantly, making her sheath tighten around his fingers. He eased them in and out but also held her clit between his teeth. With her fully confined, he licked at his leisure. She wasn't going anywhere.

Perspiration rolled down her throat, muscles quivered. Needing to hang on to something and maintain control, she tugged her hair. Didn't work. Glutted with desire, her sheath released more moisture, making it easy for him to turn his fingers within her before he pulled them out and started over, working her there while his mouth plundered, his breath warmed and his tongue tormented.

Rapture hit. Wave after wave held her within its embrace and flung her past the farthest star where she hovered over too many universes then began her descent, floating to Earth. Sex scented the room. Her sheath pulsed around his fingers and pulled them deeper.

He complied and sucked her clit.

Unendurable delight ripped through her. She would have never believed there could be too much of a good thing, however… "No, no, no." She pounded the mattress. "You're killing me."

Farron stopped tonguing her. "Angels can't die." He dipped back to her sex.

She gagged and grabbed his hair. "Stop, please. It's too much. Give me a sec to calm down. That's all I'm asking for."

"No prob." He lowered her legs, lifted his cock and plunged inside, filling her to the brim. "Take all the time you need."

She moaned wantonly. Her cunt pulsed around his stiffened rod.

Farron dropped his head, his breaths ragged, thoughts tangled. Being inside her was better than he'd dreamed, her tight heat mind-boggling. Nothing in the mortal or supernatural worlds could have held him tighter than she did, nor had he known a woman could get so wet. Ursula was positively flooded, her passion as uncontrolled as his.

His gratitude warred with good sense. Tonight's date wasn't about him going gaga. He was supposed to teach her how to be the sensual being she truly was. Boost her confidence so she could find a nice guy and live out their happily-ever-after on a damn cloud.

If another male dared touch her, he'd pulverize the jerk. No angel, man or supernatural was good enough for her.

She'd looked like a goddess on the platform, eyes gold, nipples a delicate pink, the curls between her legs the same soft brown as her hair, her curves voluptuous, like women from the past, not the stick-figures who passed for sex symbols today.

Her initial modesty had touched him in a place he hadn't realized he owned. If he'd had a heart, the thing might have swollen to ten times its normal size from the tenderness she generated within him. When she'd loosened up and masturbated herself at his request, she'd looked angelic and provocative at the same time, a killer combination. None of the porn stars he'd watched in Hell or those still on Earth had given him a better show. No other woman, and he'd had tons, had affected him as deeply as she had.

He wasn't certain why and didn't want to explore the reasons. It was enough to know she was an amazing treasure.

She fixed her gaze on him.

Her wonderfully mussed hair pointed in every direction. Her musk smelled stronger than her amber-and-honey perfume. He didn't mind, liking her natural fragrance best. His kisses had smudged her lipstick. A smear decorated her chin. He left the stain, loving her slightly ravished look, though not her puffy mouth, bruised from his zeal. He should have apologized for harming her but couldn't find enough strength to utter the words.

She'd drained his power too easily, turning him into a lovesick fool. This couldn't go on.

"Thank you." She tightened her cunt repeatedly. The hard, quick strokes squeezed his cock.

Exceptional pleasure built, encouraging him to ride her until time ended, or this impractical fantasy concluded in a few hours. He wanted to bellow his frustration at their impossible circumstances. If she'd been a demon, or if he hadn't fallen from on high, they could have chalked up today as one of a zillion moments they'd spend together. Even if they'd been mortal and facing shitty deaths, they would have had some time together.

Given their differences, they had nothing, nada, zero.

"Farron?"

He refused to open his eyes, afraid to acknowledge her or anything she had to say.

"Are you all right?"

Of course, he wasn't. If his mood nosedived even an iota farther, he'd be in tears.

She stopped squeezing his rod.

That only made things worse. He glared. "Why'd you quit?"

"Doing what?"

"Tightening your cunt around me."

Her face pinked up. "I thought you were in pain. You had this weird look on your face. Since you're okay, I'll do it again, all right?"

She flexed fast and hard.

Riotous delight shot from his shaft to his balls and bounced back. His eyebrows stood on end. "Shit. Slower. Please. I don't want to come yet."

He shouldn't come period, but couldn't help himself. If not for his bad morals, he wouldn't have had any at all.

"Sorry." She squeezed for a long moment then relaxed. "Is that better?"

Her gloved heat and snug fit were the closest things to Heaven he'd known since the Big Guy had booted him out. She was more than a warm body or tight fit...she was comfort, a home. One he suddenly craved but shouldn't. The smart thing would be to dematerialize and hide out in Hell until she forgot him.

Farron wasn't certain he had the will to banish her from his thoughts. "Yeah, keep it up. Go slow though." Drawing this out for several decades would be nice. An eternity would prove perfect...and a foolish dream. Time for him to get real, especially about no other man ever being with her. "That's what a guy likes. Don't forget that point down the road."

She lost her smile. "Down what road?"

The inevitable—her with someone else. He should have said that, but couldn't.

A sad look washed over her. She chased it away with a fast smile. "Now I know what you mean. I shouldn't forget to go slowly for you, because you like that pace. Thanks for telling me and I definitely won't pick up speed. But if I do, you'll have to remind me during all our other times. You will, right? No, wait, you don't have to answer that. Save your strength for this. I know you'll remember. I trust you completely."

Shame filled him. He wanted to crawl through the bed and floor.

Her sultry kiss and tightened cunt wouldn't allow his departure. Being a prick, he lost track of everything except his rod's slow slide in and out of her pussy, her smooth channel, ungodly hot depths and his cock slick from her moisture. The precious dew sparkled in the spotlight.

He willed the lamp to shine only where their bodies joined. Male curls touched female ones, the hues mingling. A more awesome sight didn't exist. Fainter light on her face allowed additional pigment in her hair, cheeks and eyes, the irises a perfect gold, like a tiger's.

Farron pumped ardently.

Her irises deepened in color. Her pupils dilated.

High praise, indeed, for him, revealing her enchantment. He had to give her more and rubbed her clit.

She lifted her chin to the ceiling and gripped the linen.

"Hold on to me." He slapped his biceps, showing her where.

"But my nails. I don't want to hurt you if I get carried away."

If she sliced his throat, he doubted he'd notice. His cock was too far gone, throbbing with obscene energy and thickened with need. "As long as you don't stab me with your high heels, I'm good."

She laughed.

He did, too.

With her hanging on to him, he thrust into her pussy and rubbed her clit. Each time he withdrew, she squeezed his shaft and created enough friction to make them shudder.

The bed creaked, wind rattled the window, the wall popped. He couldn't hold off. One pump blurred into the other. He and Ursula lost in their own pleasure. Groans, whimpers, grunts and shouts rang through the room.

A bellow drowned out everything. He wasn't certain if the sound came from him, her or them both.

His cum spurted and his chest pumped hard. Woozy, he swayed.

She reached for him. "Don't fall."

He'd already done so, metaphorically, and look where that sorry decision had landed him. Between an angel's legs, an extraordinary woman he wanted to keep. Fighting his idiotic desire, he pushed up and sagged down, unsteady as hell.

"Relax." She gathered him to her and guided his head to her breasts.

No pillow had ever been softer or smelled as good.

"Sleep." She stroked his back. "When you wake up, we'll…"

He drifted off.

Chapter Seven

Ursula finger-combed Farron's hair and chattered endlessly, as if he was awake rather than unconscious in her arms. "Then after we finish visiting Europe, since we're here already, we can check out the US, especially California. I've never been to Universal Studios Hollywood. I hear it's amazing, particularly the Jurassic Park thing. Oh, we should also go to Six Flags Magic Mountain. Their rides look scary, but with you holding me, I won't be afraid."

He snored softly.

She fell silent and stilled, too, uncertain what she should do now. If she'd had a cell phone, she would have called Constance for advice. Farron's phone would work, if Ursula knew where his clothes had gone. They weren't in the suite. Hers, either, which presented a problem. Unlike him, she couldn't conjure up stuff from thin air, especially the confidence she needed.

He was going to dump her. His down-the-road comment hadn't fooled her in the least and she hadn't a clue what she'd done to deserve it. She'd posed nude for him on the pedestal, played with herself, even considered voyeurism in the future, and he still planned to cut out when tonight ended.

Tears pricked her eyes, her emotions raw and unsure. Some women might have berated her for being too needy, telling her to buck up, pull on her big girl pants and move on. No guy was worth crying over.

Maybe not, but it was easy to talk big when you had nothing to lose. When you'd never spent a life then an eternity alone and unwanted, longing for a smidge of affection and a gaze meant for you alone. Farron had given her that, showing what life could be like sharing her days with a man she loved. One who wanted her in return. No one, not even him, could convince her that his desire was put on or lacking.

She hugged him as hard as she could.

He made a questioning sound that could have been "huh?" or "what?" then settled back to sleep, content and untroubled.

She wished she could be as casual. Unable to, she had two choices—go with the flow and accept whatever happened then slink away like a beaten animal when things tanked, or fight for her man and seduce the fuck out of him as Constance had advised.

Not much of a decision.

She eased him to the comforter and rolled off the mattress. He choked on a snore, coughed then stilled, his legs and arms flung out, cock impressive, tempting her. Endlessly, she ached for him, though not because he was a drool-worthy hunk. She liked his teasing the most. His protective nature was awesome too. His lovemaking straight from a steamy romance. No matter what he thought of himself, he was a good soul, better than many angels she knew. They used their superior status to make others feel less worthy, believing they had a corner on righteousness.

What fools they were. Farron could have taught them how a real man and angel should behave.

She backed away slowly, not wanting him to wake just yet. If he got up too soon, he'd ruin her surprise. If he took off while she was out of the room, she'd never get over the pain. She stopped several feet away, her chest and stomach cramping at him possibly abandoning her.

No, he wasn't cruel. He'd at least bring her back to the service...or send someone here to escort her there.

Queasy with worry, she needed to make a decision and hurried to the master bath. The ceiling rivaled the Sistine Chapel in grandeur, colorful frescoes of half-naked women and plump cherubs glancing down at the opulent room. This place had more white-and-pink marble than a quarry. She switched on the monstrous chandelier, opened the drapes over five windows and bypassed the Olympic-size Jacuzzi in favor of the glass-enclosed shower, spacious enough to accommodate an Italian rugby team.

The banker who owned this place knew how to live. She figured he was a greedy SOB who would probably end up in Hell.

After spritzing perfume, she grabbed bath oil scented with apple, nutmeg, vanilla and cinnamon. If nothing else, this place would soon smell like the Marie Callender's pie she'd bought at the supermarket. She flung the oils onto the shower walls and floor, the rosy stone veined with white. Once the water was on full blast, she directed the four heads so the spray hit the oil, after which she jacked up the temperature to boiling.

Steam rose and plumes spilled over the door. The glass fogged. *Amazing* didn't adequately describe the fragrance.

Ready for anything, except rejection, she turned the dial to a lower heat. After removing her heels and earrings, she tested the flow, found it pleasantly warm, and slipped inside. Her view beyond the glass was hazy, but she could see well enough to detect movement.

There wasn't any…yet.

She adjusted the spray to hit her full-on, the flow resembling raindrops, then lathered her hair with shampoo and her bod with soap.

Still no movement.

Hopefully, the water heaters were large enough to keep the drizzle toasty for several hours. Who knew how long Farron would snooze?

She washed her hair twice, her other parts three times, her pace slow then sluggish. Her fingers and toes wrinkled. Maybe this hadn't been such a good idea. The bubbling Jacuzzi might have awakened him sooner.

Then again…

A blurry figure lumbered into the room. She prayed it was Farron, not another demon he'd sent to fetch and take her back. Unwilling to believe such a horrible thing, she slathered shampoo on her hair and snuck peeks at the door.

He'd disappeared.

Her throat tightened.

He couldn't have dragged back to bed or worse, dematerialized to avoid a 'this is about me, not you' breakup scene. She darted to the right and the left then stood on tiptoes and struggled to check out the room.

A hand smacked the shower door.

She jumped back and squinted, hoping to make out details—an arm, leg, cock, face. No such luck. Everything was a steamy haze, the blob indistinct.

The door rattled then flew open.

Farron's hair stuck to his forehead from the oppressive humidity. His shoulders were slumped, eyes hooded, the hickey she'd given him on one pec fire-engine red and wider than Texas. Yawning loudly, he joined her in the shower, closed the door behind him and scrubbed his face with his hands. "I smell apple pie. Did you order some?"

"Is there a kitchen staff in the villa?"

"No. I meant from a restaurant or conjuring up a slice."

"I'm not at a level where I can materialize stuff." She'd been stuck in admin hell for centuries.

He sniffed. "Where'd the odors come from?"

"Oils."

"What oils? What are you doing in here?"

"Pleasuring you."

She had him now. He was too tired to bolt, too confused to argue and too aroused to resist her pressed to him. His shaft blossomed and snuggled against her delicate curls. She forced him to the back wall. His shoulders and ass tapped the marble. He looked over and grabbed the gold towel rods on either side.

Give her two sets of handcuffs he couldn't break out of and she'd be a happy camper. "Don't move."

He sagged against the wall, his chin raised. Water streamed down him. "Why?"

"It's not easy to lather a moving target."

He laughed wearily.

She smeared bubbles on his pecs, shoulders, his tat and the silky hair in his pits.

He squirmed. "That tickles."

"Is this better?" She ran soap down his rod. It came alive at her touch, hotter than the sun, harder than stone, thicker than the soupy air in here.

He pushed to his toes. "Uh…"

With her hands on his narrow hips, she sank down and knelt before him as he deserved. He was the most magnificent creature she'd ever known. More importantly, he was a good and kind man. Nothing like the image he'd portrayed in the hall when he'd attacked Heather. That was his uncertainty coming out. He'd masked it with exaggerated masculinity and mindless lust.

This evening, he'd shown her the real Farron and Ursula couldn't have been more impressed. He was her world and future if he'd only allow that.

Her sweeping touch took in his ass, thighs and nuts.

He grunted indelicately.

She cradled his boys with honor and care then pressed her face to his raven curls. A contented sound spilled from him. She trembled in delight. The water hadn't washed away his musk, a fragrance that made her fevered and wanting.

With great care, she fondled his boys and tugged his short and curlies with her teeth.

He chuckled. "You're something."

She was an angel in love. "You don't like?"

"I didn't say that. Don't put words in my mouth."

"No, sir. This will have to do in mine." She slipped his cock between her lips.

Air hissed through his teeth.

What a beautiful sound. His pre-cum wasn't bad either. She adored the faint saltiness but couldn't tarry when she had so much to do. Recalling the torrid romances she'd read, Ursula opened her throat and took him in, inch by spectacular inch, until her nose rested against his fragrant thatch.

He cried out joyously.

When he was with her, she wanted him to know nothing except delight. Still cupping his balls in one hand, she explored his ass and stroked his anus with the other.

He groaned. "Fuck, fuck, fuck."

In time, they would, all day and night, each minute and hour through eternity. She had to win the unspoken battle they waged and keep him at her side. Slowly, she eased his shaft from her mouth until only his crown remained between her lips. The same as the heroine had done with her four guys in *Wanton Wicked Secrets*, the second book in the *Scandalous Secrets* series. Devilishly, Ursula flicked her tongue against the bumpy skin at the back of his head.

He shuddered and groaned. Proof that was a man's most sensitive part, just as the book had claimed.

She licked him, squeezed his balls gently and worked her little finger into his tightest passage.

"Holy mother fuck, you're killing me." He writhed away then returned for more.

She let his cock slip from her lips. "Fallen angels can't die." Giving him no chance to retort, she eased his right testicle into her mouth.

He groaned lustily and pushed into her.

She couldn't blame him. This was amazing, his skin wonderfully furred, precisely as a man's should be.

How dare Anatol suggest manscaping. Not one hair was out of place on Farron. She licked him greedily.

Bestial noises burst from him that might have scared her if she hadn't known what a sweetie he could be. Even the crude oaths he sputtered sounded musical and gentle. When his curses didn't calm him, he rattled the towel rods and bounced on his heels.

She followed his movements to keep from losing her hold on his nut and sucked it carefully but vigorously.

He shouted so loudly the glass doors and walls rattled.

Unfazed, she finished with his boy, slipped the other into her mouth and grabbed his shaft then worked it with her hand as her pussy would.

"*Hell, hell, fucking hell.* This is too much."

They'd only begun. She probed his anus again.

He tore a rack from the wall. The metal clanged on the marble floor. Water drenched them and steam caressed, creating a wanton world she never wanted to leave.

After another suck, she let his ball escape her mouth and took in his rod. This time, she didn't fool around, gliding him in and out, licking his pleasure zone, sucking, probing, loving.

He came on a thunderous shout. The glass cracked and the water halted for a moment, then rained down on them once more.

His creamy, rich cum spilled into her mouth, its flavor dark and delicious, better than the *Mont Blanc* at the restaurant. She drank greedily, adoring everything about him.

Gasping, he slumped against the wall, arms limp at his sides.

She finished lapping him clean and guided him to the damp floor.

He draped his arm over his eyes.

She straddled him. "You're still hard." His rigid shaft pressed against the furrow between her cheeks, defying gravity again. "Do I make you that way...or did I do something wrong?"

He huffed. "What did I tell you about downing yourself?"

"I forget."

He pulled her down and pinned her to him with one arm.

She squealed.

He spanked her, the smacks loud in the enclosed space, the sting minimal, heat heavenly. She wiggled into him. "Don't stop. Ever."

He did, puffing worse than she did. "Tell me you're beautiful."

"Why? Don't you already know?"

He swatted her again. "Say the words. No screwing around."

"That's the best part."

He laughed.

She pushed up. "I'm beautiful because you think so. That's all that matters to me. Don't move."

He didn't, not even to open his eyes and meet her gaze. Again, he was running from her and avoiding intimacy.

If Ursula truly believed he didn't like her, she would have taken off, licked her wounds and forced herself to forget him. She didn't want to be a burden to anyone, especially if that person didn't like her.

Farron did. Affection had shone in his eyes more times than she could count. Desire rang in his voice and showed in his every move. Like now. His cock tapped her buttocks. Proof he was falling as much as she had.

On her knees, she directed his shaft to her puffy folds and slipped the crown inside. A delicate shudder rolled through her. Paradise could never beat this.

His lids fluttered open, his eyes hazy with passion, his complexion darkening. Water beaded on his lashes and eyebrows. He held her hips and stroked her gently.

His response to her touch told her the only truth she needed to know.

With more grace then she believed she had, she glided down his thick column, her sheath swallowing his rod.

He grinned at the sight, his dimples the deepest ever. A gift she'd hold in her heart forever. "What now?"

He looked up. "What do you think? Have you forgotten everything I taught you?"

She'd burned their moments into her soul. "Never. I meant, fast, slow, hard, soft?"

"What do you want?"

Forever, with him beside her. A chance at a real future, not simply an existence. Unparalleled happiness and confidence they'd always be together. "Let's find out." She wiggled, making sure he was as deep as he could go, then rose slowly. Her channel tightened around him to provide maximum resistance.

He gripped her hips.

She flexed her inner muscles.

Lust, tenderness and what might have been beginning love swept over his face. His eyes flamed more than they ever had.

Returning his adoring gaze, she rode him slowly and long. The water had grown coolish, a relief, actually. Never had she been as warm. Perspiration mingled with water, her sex and his joined, their skin's gentle tapping a love song.

They came at last, as one, their shouts blending. The same as their shared days ahead.

Weary, she sagged to him.

He greeted her with a prolonged embrace, a searching kiss and finally a sigh.

Words weren't necessary. She'd won.

Ursula woke in bed, not having recalled leaving the shower or falling asleep. The candles were out, every light off, curtains and drapes pulled back. A fat moon brightened the suite, ashy rays defining shapes.

Fully clothed, Farron faced the window. Her dress, bra and thong lay on a throne-like chair to his side, her shoes and earrings on a gilt-edged table.

Her chest ached. They couldn't be leaving, their evening over already. She'd won the battle, making him as happy as she was.

Maybe he was bored with this place and wanted to zip somewhere else — the Pyramids, Mount Everest, his places in Hell. Wherever he planned to go, she'd follow. Propped on her elbows, she pushed up. The mattress squeaked.

He looked over.

In the gloom, she couldn't determine his mood, but his eyes terrified her. The flames were mere pinpoints, horribly subdued, not the lusty beast she'd come to know and love. "Where are we going now? Venice? Antarctica? Cabo? A mall or outdoor market? I hear the ones in Baja are fun. No set prices. You haggle over everything. Sometimes you win. Sometimes the vendors do. Everyone has a great time. Is the moon real or did you do that?"

"It's three a.m. here."

"Great. Time for bed." She patted the mattress. "Come on. Let's have some —"

In a flash, she was dressed, no longer in bed but seated in the ornate chair, large enough for King Kong. Her feet dangled above the floor. She scooted off the seat, her stomach hurting. "Where are we going now?"

He regarded the view. Roman ruins, the Arch of Constantine, and the Colosseum got his attention, not her. "I have business to attend to."

"Now? Someone called you to work?"

"This is stuff I had to do before I left."

Surely not a demonic possession. He wouldn't do that to an innocent soul. He was a good guy. "How long will your stuff take?"

"I need to get you back." He didn't look at her. "Ready?"

She blinked. Already they were in an empty treatment room at the service, their date over, destiny unsettled. "Wait. Are you going to call me, email or text when you're through with your work? Let me give you my info."

Looking past her, he backed away. "I'll be busy for some time. I have to go."

He was gone. No flash, smoke, goodbye kiss, nothing.

Excruciating loss gripped her. Doubled over from the pain, she lifted her face and sniffed, hoping to catch his scent, but didn't. It was as if he'd never existed, their night together a dream with her awakening into a nightmare. He couldn't have had a bad time. She refused to believe that but didn't understand why he'd changed.

Or maybe she did understand. While she'd slept, Becca must have called him. Ursula gritted her teeth.

Even if Becca meant well, she had no damn right to interfere and wouldn't again. They were going to have a talk.

A large mirror near the door stopped Ursula. Panicked, she backed away from her reflection and flicked on the lights. That only made things worse. She doused the fluorescent beams and dragged to the mirror, afraid to look but had no choice.

Her irises weren't light hazel any longer, but pure gold, like coins from the Franklin Mint. Rather pretty. Deeply disturbing, too, if this wasn't Farron's way of marking her as she'd done with him and the hickey. She leaned forward and gasped then squinted. The flames she thought she'd seen sputter in her pupils weren't there now, though they might be later.

Afraid someone might ask what had happened to her, she searched drawers for the industrial-strength sunglasses the service provided weres. They used the protective shades when they hadn't yet graduated therapy but wanted to take their gals out on moonlit nights. The mortal women had dug the look that made their bad boys even hotter.

She slipped on a pair and had to wait for her eyes to adjust to the dark. Didn't happen. Legally, she was blind, but had to get to Becca's office for her regular clothes and a talk. She tottered down the hall, batting air. Her palm landed on something firm yet soft. Curious, she squeezed.

"Hi to you, too." Wynona brushed aside Ursula's hand. "How'd your date go?"

"Where are my clothes?"

"You're wearing them. I don't want to know if you took them off."

"That. Is. It. Farron's a nice guy." She grabbed Wynona's hair and tugged hard. "Don't you ever say anything bad about him, got it?"

"Easy, princess." She dug her nails into Ursula's wrists until she let go. "That's better. Why the shades? Are you hungover?" She sniffed. "Why do you smell like apple pie?"

"I need my clothes and to talk to Becca. Is she here yet?"

"Right next to me."

Ursula patted air and connected with bare skin then something hard and dangling. She guessed Becca's navel jewelry.

Becca stepped back. "Why did you need to talk to me?"

Surely, she was joking. "How dare you call Farron and tell him not to date me. What right do you have to interfere in my life?"

"Ah, none, though I do worry about you. But I didn't call him. The last time we spoke was right before you two took off. Did he say I called?"

"No. He was so—then he wasn't—then he did—but later he didn't—and…" She couldn't go on. Her throat convulsed from sorrow.

"Uh-huh." Becca made a pained sound. "Let's talk in the break room. We won't turn on the lights. You can take off your shades."

"No, I need to talk to him. What's the number for Hell?"

Dead freaking silence.

"Fine. I'll look in his file." She pivoted and ran into something hard.

"Hey, didn't know you were back." Daemon made chewing sounds. "You're okay, right? Farron didn't do anything to you?"

He'd changed her existence, making each unbearably long day worthwhile. If Becca hadn't called him, there was no reason for his behavior, unless…

She recalled their shower and bed play. Maybe she hadn't been wild enough for him. Could be he'd really wanted an audience and she'd denied him that by being such a prude.

Stupid, stupid, stupid. When would she learn to loosen up? "I gotta call him."

"First, tell us what happened." Becca took her arm.

Someone else, possibly Wynona, took her other one. Together they pulled her down the hall and into a room. A door closed. Chair legs scraped.

"Go on, sit."

Despite Wynona's pleasant offer, Ursula didn't budge.

"Hon, take off the shades. It's so dark in here, we can't see."

She whipped them off but kept her face down.

Becca edged close, her toe rings and ankle bracelets gleaming dully. "I don't want to pry."

"Good."

"Uh-huh. Are your wings okay?"

Ursula unfurled them. Becca and Wynona's relieved sighs broke the quiet, proving what she'd already guessed. Her feathers were still white.

"Sweetie." Becca took her hands. "It's just as well you didn't get too involved with Farron. You sleeping with — that is, getting too close to him wouldn't have been the right choice. You were wise to have kept your head."

She laughed.

Wynona touched her shoulder. "You okay?"

She was dying, even though angels couldn't do that. "I slept with him near the Colosseum, not far from where I was buried alive. We showered so long my fingers and toes are still wrinkly. That's why I smell like pie. He put me on a pedestal, literally, and evaporated my clothes and spanked me when I said *dull* instead of *clit*. I love him." She buried her face in her hands.

Chair legs scraped again. Given the sound, both women had sat down hard.

"Oh, sweetie." Becca squeezed Ursula's elbow. "Are you sure you're okay? Did he give you something to drink? Drugs maybe?"

"I'm not drunk or high. I'm dying here." She dropped her hands and lifted her face.

They gaped.

Becca's hand flew to her chest. "Oh, my God, what happened to your eyes?"

She had to be joking. Only Farron could have managed this change in her. "What do you think?"

Wynona squinted. "Are those flames? Did he possess you? Is he like inside you?" She made a face and turned to Becca. "We need an exorcist. Surely, Rafael knows a good one. I'm still a newbie up there. I'll text him pronto and we'll get this show on the road."

"No, we won't." Ursula pointed at Wynona's chair. "Sit. Down."

"You can't mean that. It must be Farron talking. Tell him to knock it off. Better yet, tell him to get lost. It's got to be crowded as hell with the two of you in the same bod."

"He's not inside me. Hell, I wish he were. His cock in his pussy." There, she'd said the nasty words and hadn't been struck dead. This was worse. She felt more awful than when she'd died in the *Campus Sceleratus*. "He took off to go to work. Everything was fine until I fell asleep then bam, I wake up and he couldn't wait to leave our villa."

"He took you to an Italian villa?" Wynona tapped her chin. "I have to admit, I'm impressed. Wouldn't have ever thought he'd be that smooth. Maybe the treatments here are working." She pointed. "You really shouldn't have fallen asleep on him while he was doing the deed. Guys don't like that."

"No kidding and I didn't. We both passed out after I went down on him. Wait. I rode him hard first."

Becca made a face. "Do you know what all that means?"

"I've read dozens of triple X-rated romances Wynona gave me. So, yeah, I know what it means. It was great. He enjoyed it. I did too. What's the problem? No, don't tell me. We're from different worlds. I don't care. I want him."

She left the room and grabbed the closest computer she could find. After a brief file search, she had Farron's number. The first call rang once and went to voicemail. So, did the next ten. Uncertain what to say, she didn't leave any messages. She tried email next, with a simple "hi, it's me" as the message. The email bounced back, the error permanent with no explanation as to why. She sent him one text message, again a simple "hi."

He didn't answer.

She told herself he was busy.

The day passed more slowly than the countless others Ursula had known. Thankfully, she was numb, her panic and anguish held at bay. Hour by hour, her emotional fog dissipated, leaving nothing but raw heartache. It hurt so much she could scarcely breathe.

Daemon offered her his Milky Ways and Hostess cupcakes, along with a gentle smile. "Youi should eat. Chocolate always makes me feel better."

Any food did that for him. "Thanks, but I'm not hungry."

Heather hugged her repeatedly and smoothed her hair. "Things will get better, you'll see."

Easy for an upbeat good fairy to say, especially when she already had her guy.

Constance lifted her hands. "Say the word and I'll remove those terrible memories from you. You'll never know Farron existed."

"I have a better thought." MJ squeezed Ursula's shoulder. "Make a wish for him to not exist any longer and it's yours. Promise. He'll be toast."

Ursula bolted down the hall and locked herself in a treatment room away from their horrible suggestions. Unfortunately, a vamp was in there, his treatments just begun, his fangs elongating, eyes focused on her like a cat stalking prey.

He pounced.

Zoe stormed inside, yanked the guy off Ursula and rammed her elbow into his belly.

He screamed.

Taro, Anatol and Stefin threw him back on the table and restrained him with countless straps.

Zoe escorted Ursula to the hall. "If you have to go somewhere other than Wynona's office, always use the room over there." She pointed. "It's empty. I promise no one will bother you and you won't bother them."

"How well do you know Farron? You're both demons. You must know everything about him."

"Sorry, but no. Do you know every angel in Heaven?"

There were far too many. She plodded to the other room and tried contacting him repeatedly. Nothing.

Days later, her hurt was gone replaced by steely determination. She stormed into Becca's office. "You need to help me. I want to go to Hell."

Chapter Eight

The ocean churned restlessly in the expansive view surrounding Farron's desk. Salt spray tanged the air. An illusion. Behind the sailboats and females sunbathing in the nude, brimstone smoldered.

He changed the scene to a flowering meadow, tall grass peppered with poppies and buttercups, towering mountains in the distance, their bluish-gray peaks capped with snow. Naked women lounged on towels near a sparkling lake, baking their flesh in the brilliant sun.

Each time he switched the landscape, the same babes frolicked, once in a gentle rain then a blizzard. Even with the temperature below freezing, they wore nothing except furry UGG boots. Their boobs bounced merrily, the thatch between their legs dusted with flakes that resembled powdered sugar.

"Interesting."

At his secretary's comment, he looked over. Gigi wore a leather body harness, long on straps, short on coverage, her breasts and cunt exposed. A surprisingly demure outfit given her usual fetish wear that included nipple clamps and labia rings. Young and sultry, she resembled Scarlett Johansson right down to her blue eyes and blonde hair.

Indifferent, he turned away. "What's interesting?"

She joined him and pointed her pen at the women building a snowman. "Their faces are the same."

What do you know? Each had pouty lips, flushed cheeks and gold eyes. In other words, Ursula's features. He yearned so badly for her, he couldn't draw a breath. He killed the image and exposed the glowing rock. "You're here because…"

"You have a call on line one." She inclined her head to the blinking button on his phone. Line three.

Gigi wasn't the brightest bulb in the pack. He'd hired her as eye candy and let his other staff do the real work. "Care to tell me who?"

"Some woman who keeps apologizing for calling."

He went hotter than he already was, grew cold then sweltered again. "Did she criticize herself, too?"

Ursula had better not. He'd promised her another spanking if she did, but that was never going to happen. They were history, their night together too intense, leading nowhere. At last, he'd understood he couldn't fuck up her existence as he had his. He'd fallen on his sword for her and wanted to pulverize something.

He glared at Gigi. "Did she say she was frumpy and uninteresting?"

"Can't recall. I stopped listening to her babble. Somewhere in there she did say she was From Studly Crudly or something like that."

The blinking phone beckoned him like Excedrin extra-strength after a gallon of absinthe. He gripped his chair, refusing to answer. Ursula must have gotten his office number in his file. He'd blocked her calls and texts from his personal smartphone and deleted his Yahoo! email account in anticipation of her contacting him, but hadn't considered doing the same for this place. "Tell her I'm out for the next century on important business. No, wait." She'd want to leave a message he might not be strong enough to resist. "Hang up. If she calls back, pretend you made a mistake then hang up again until she quits calling."

How long that might take was a mystery. He tensed, uncertain whether Ursula forgetting him would hurt worse than him having to dodge her. The adult thing was to tell her they had no future without mincing words.

He wasn't that mature or brave. "Tell her I got married and I'm on a decade-long cruise."

It was mean but would be a clean break rather than a festering wound neither of them needed.

Gigi wobbled away on her thigh-high platform boots. "Got it."

That'd be a first. "Stop." He worried what she might say. With her, the garbled message might give Ursula the idea that she and Gigi were getting hitched. "Take the call here. I'll help if you run into trouble."

She brightened. "Do you want to take it first and show me how so I don't mess up?"

He slumped, wearier than he'd ever been. "Nope. While you're on the phone, pretend I'm not here…to the caller."

"Got it."

He hoped.

She hopped on his desk, long legs crossed. With the receiver to her ear, she punched the wrong button. "Hi, I'm back. Farron's…" She stopped and looked at him. "She hung up."

"She's back." He pointed to the still-flashing button.

"Wow, that was fast. I didn't even hear it ring." Gigi depressed the button. "Hi, you still there?" She listened briefly and rolled her eyes. "No need to apologize. I—"

He pressed the button, putting the call back on hold. "Ditch the marriage thing. Ask her what she wants." If Ursula was in trouble with the powers-that-be because of their date, and needed his help, he'd never forgive himself for ignoring her. He'd be no better than the pricks who'd buried her alive, leaving her frightened and alone, then dead. "Go on."

"This is hard."

She had no idea.

Back on the phone, Gigi spoke fast. "Hey there, back again. Before you say anything, want do you want?" She listened and nodded. "Let me check." She put the receiver between her breasts.

Before she could speak, he put the call on hold. "What?"

"She wants to know if you'd mind rescheduling your appointment. She double-booked or something and you'll be in the same room with a bear."

A were. The call wasn't from Ursula. Heather was the one apologizing ceaselessly. Disappointment battered him. He slouched then told himself he was nuts for feeling anything except relief. "Cancel my appointment. Tell her I've changed my mind. I'm not coming back."

"You got it."

He grabbed Gigi's wrist before she could lift the receiver from her boobs. "Ask her if Ursula's okay. Wait. Don't say anything about her. Fuck. Tell her you only want to know if Ursula's all right and if the goons upstairs haven't come down hard on her because of — no, don't go into that. Say you don't want her, Ursula, to know I'm — we're — you're asking. It has to be a secret between the two of you. Heather and you. Not you and Ursula. Even Becca can't know. Especially Becca. Think you can do that?"

"No. Can you write it down?"

He did. But only that he was cancelling all future appointments and wouldn't be coming back. He jabbed his finger at his script. "Tell her what you see here."

Before Gigi could, he left his office for the first of many drinks this day.

* * * *

Ursula wasn't going to let Farron get away with this. If he hated her, she wanted to hear the words. If she bored him, he'd have to tell her. To. Her. Face. No pussyfooting around any longer. She deserved an answer and demanded action. "Did you hear what I said?"

Becca's hand was to her forehead, face down. "I'm still trying to digest it."

"Then you can't help me. Is that what you're not saying? Or are you refusing to help?"

She glared right back. "Since I've never wanted to step foot in Hell, I don't know how to get there, all right?"

"A demon would." Finished with being a wuss, Ursula leaned over Becca's desk and buzzed Zoe.

"Yo."

"In Becca's office. Now."

"Ursula?"

"I. Said. Now." She tapped her foot and waited.

Several minutes later, Becca buzzed Zoe. "Can you come in here? Please?"

Ursula lifted her chin. "You need to be more forceful with your staff."

"Like you are?"

Ursula met Zoe at the door, then closed and locked it behind her. "How do I get to Hell?"

Zoe stared. "You're a good angel and you don't know the ins-and-outs of damnation? Seriously?"

"I'm not talking everlasting doom. I'm referring to physically visiting there. You know, like a trip to Disney World."

"That it's not. Are you feeling all right? I see your eyes haven't gotten any better. Whoa, are those flames?" Zoe leaned in and shook her head. "Not there any longer. Must have been the light playing tricks. I didn't ask days ago, but maybe I should have. You did the deed with Farron, huh?"

"And a whole lot more. I'm not ashamed."

"Different strokes."

"How do I get to Hell? And don't you dare say I've already been there with him."

"Wouldn't think of it." She looked at Becca. "Is this a joke?"

"I wish it were. But no, tell her."

She shrugged. "Do the obvious. Off good people, puppies and kittens. Start a war. Steal old ladies' retirement funds. Price fix cable and internet service, while slowing down the download speeds. Jack up prescription medicine costs. Or sell your soul like I did.

Dumbest mistake I ever made. And for Ebenezer, of all people. What a freaking louse. Satan, too. Talk about bait and switch. That prick—"

"No, no, no." Ursula shook Zoe. "I want to visit, not stay."

Flames erupted in Zoe's eyes. Smoke puffed from her hair and shoulders.

Becca ground her hand into her forehead. "Ursula, a little advice. Calm down unless you want to be incinerated."

She tightened her grip, jaw clenched. "Angels can't die."

"Fine. But you won't get an answer unless you chill."

She smoothed the wrinkles she'd put in Zoe's silk blouse, a nice maroon shade to match her heated cheeks. "Sorry. Please help me."

"Why? I don't understand any of this."

Becca sighed. "None of us do, but she wants to go to Hell to see Farron."

Zoe made a face.

Ursula would have smacked her but heeded Becca's words and restrained herself. "Will you help me?"

"Why not wait for his next appointment? He's booked for every Wednesday and Friday into infinity or until he becomes civilized. Whichever comes first."

"He'll be here tomorrow then." Becca pressed her intercom. "Let me get the scheduled time. Heather?"

"Hi. I would've answered faster, but I was working on the accounts. Sorry. It won't happen again. Sorry."

"No prob. When is Farron expected for tomorrow's appointment?"

"He isn't. He canceled. Or rather his girl did."

Ursula rushed to Becca's desk, her insides cramping. "What girl?"

"Oh, hi, Ursula. Sorry, I meant to say the girl who answers his phone. I should have been clearer. Really, I'm sorry. I don't know her name. I should have asked. Please forgive me for not doing so. She did sound nice, even though she put me on hold numerous — "

"She rescheduled for him?" Ursula gripped the phone hard enough to make the plastic groan. "What day will he be here?"

"Never. I'm sorry. This is my fault."

"How? What do you mean never?"

"I double-booked and called him to reschedule, but he didn't want to. She, his employee, said he wasn't coming back."

Ursula sagged against the desk.

Heather made a pained sound. "I tried to find out if I'd angered him by rescheduling or why he wouldn't want more sessions considering how he, uh, is at times, but she wasn't clear on his reasons. Something about cruising into the next decade and a hang-up or hanging up. I didn't want to be rude and ask what she meant. Maybe I should have been more forceful. I'm so sorry."

"S'okay." Becca killed the connection and stroked Ursula's fist. "I know this doesn't help much, but we've all been where you are. Before I met Eric, I liked tons of guys and they all dumped me."

Zoe snorted. "At least you didn't sell your soul for any of them. Even my everlasting damnation didn't get Ebenezer to notice me. Jerk."

"That's you two, not me." Ursula pulled her hand from Becca's. "I know when a man's disinterested. All of them have been except for Farron. Rafael never once looked at me as he does Wynona. But Farron has. Either he wants me or he's the greatest actor since time began or he's simply a creep who did this to be mean."

Zoe exchanged a look with Becca. "I choose door number three."

"Wrong." Ursula got in Zoe's face.

Zoe bunched her shoulders. Smoke billowed from them and her hair.

Becca held up her hand. "Easy, ladies. Ursula, did you ever consider a fourth option? That Farron realizes there's no future in this and he doesn't want to hurt you?"

She hoped that wasn't true. It would destroy her. "So, he's given up without even trying, thinking that wouldn't wound me more?"

"Sweetie, this isn't in the cards. A good angel and demon has never been done before."

Then she and Farron would have to be the first. Anything was possible. Even the blackest soul could be redeemed, and Farron's couldn't be much worse than light gray. He had more goodness in his little finger than she had in her entire bod. If anyone stood in her way on this, she'd tear them apart. "I want him — not you — to tell me that we're doomed." She batted away Zoe's smoke and spoke to her. "Will you bring me down there so I can talk to him?"

"At his office in front of everyone?" She shook her head. "You don't want to do that."

"Fine. We'll go to wherever he lives."

"Last I heard he had a penthouse at one of his clubs."

"What?" She jabbed Zoe's shoulder. "Before when we talked, you said you didn't know anything about him."

Zoe pushed Ursula's hand away. "You asked if I knew *everything* about him and I told you no, because I don't."

"But you heard he has a penthouse. That has to be one of his places." She recalled what Salem had said at the restaurant and how quickly Farron had cut him off. "Are his clubs like the Playboy mansion?"

Zoe laughed. The deep, throaty sound cracked a window. "Way worse, but better, too, if you know what I mean. Farron owns the baddest BDSM clubs in the second circle, twelve by last count. Those places have stuff the others can only dream of doing. It's all in *Hell Fire,* the weekly rag. He's the wealthiest dude down there, except for Satan."

Funny how much she knew about Farron when she'd said she didn't, which made her exactly like the others here — intrusive, bossy and determined that Ursula forget him. No freaking way. "Then he's not into possessions?"

"Says who? He wears designer duds, has nice digs, a Maserati, Ferrari and Rolls. Nothing ostentatious, all classy. Strange, considering he comes on so strong with the babes."

That's because he hadn't found the right woman until he'd met her. "I'm not talking about stuff. I meant demonic possession. He doesn't do that?"

"He's into entertainment, not torture. Except for what goes on in his clubs, but that's role-playing. No one gets hurt."

Ursula grinned so hard her cheeks ached. He was a good guy, just as she thought. "Take me there. I want to see everything and him."

Becca groaned. "One look at that place and you'll freak out, not to mention what happens to the others there when they see you."

"Look, I know I'm not beautiful, no matter what he said, but I'm not a ghoul. They'll hardly turn into blocks of salt."

"Did I say that? You're gorgeous, but you're a good angel. You positively reek of purity."

"Not my eyes." She widened them.

Becca threw up her hands.

"You can't go like that." Zoe gestured to Ursula's office wear. A high-collared blouse, boxy suit jacket, longish skirt and sensible heels, the ensemble in varying shades of gray. "Everyone will think you're selling salvation and will run for the exits."

"So, I'll wear my leather dress from the date and those killer heels."

"Too demure."

That didn't seem possible. She pressed her thighs together. "Naked?"

"Too passé. I can't explain as well as a picture can." She touched Becca's laptop. "Mind if I use this for show and tell?"

"You can't imagine, but go on. I have a sinking feeling nothing's going to stop her."

Becca had that right.

"Are we going to watch porn that takes place at his clubs? Does he film movies there?"

"Not that I know of, but there's a thought. You should bring it up when you see him." Zoe keyed briefly then turned the screen. "Mind you, these are just some of the things you could wear down there."

Wasn't much. Rings, clamps, red or black leather strips with numerous zippers, buckles and spikes, the hardware being larger than the animal skins. "Are those pieces of the outfit? Do I have to put them together, like construct them?"

"Each of those babies can be and usually is the total outfit sans ball gags, cuffs, whips and possibly a chastity belt."

"Ew. Why would anyone wear a chastity belt in the second circle?"

"Because a Dom insists on it. You're his possession to do with as he wills." She smacked Ursula's butt.

Warmth shot through her. She trembled.

Becca narrowed her eyes. "You're about to come, aren't you?"

She definitely had to work on her poker face as Farron had suggested. "I can do this. Which one of these should I wear and when do we leave?"

Zoe scrolled down the screen. "Since you're new at this, we'll be cautious. Let's go for the female slave harness, the orgasmic belt and extreme boots. Remember that, *extreme*."

Like anything was normal on this site?

The first item was a brutal collar with thick leather straps worn beneath a woman's breasts and around her waist, leaving her essentially naked. The purchaser could choose the thing in black or red. The belt was in black only, worn low on the hips. It held a small dildo to a woman's clit. Batteries not included.

Zoe tapped the screen. "Each step and that baby hums, sending you over the rainbow."

Perspiration ran down Ursula's back.

The platform boots were black with spikes, zippers and stilt-like heels. "Won't these make me taller than him?"

"Naw, you're safe."

Not in that outfit I wouldn't be. "What about the capes?" She pointed. "I can wear that long one over the other stuff until we get to Farron's penthouse, right?"

"Sorry, no. Since you've never been to Hell before, guards will frisk you at the gate. No way to keep your cape during that."

Her dignity, either.

Becca rocked in her chair, her face smug. "Change your mind?"

"No."

"Wonderful." Her sour look said otherwise. "What do you intend to do about your wings?"

"Don't worry, I'll keep them tucked away." Unless... She looked at Zoe. "Will the guards frisk them?"

"Just your boobs, ass and pussy." She chuckled. "Those guys. Always horsing around."

Ursula crossed her arms protectively.

"You're forgetting the seams in your back." Becca arched one eyebrow. "You know, the ones where your wings come out. What are you going to do about them?"

"They're only two thin lines. Not that noticeable."

"Uh, maybe so." Zoe's chewed her thumb. "That spotlight the guards use is pretty potent."

What's with demons? They come from the dark side but never do anything in the gloom? "Can we use makeup to cover them?"

"Nope. Tats."

"I have to get a tattoo?"

"Two of them. The temporary kind that peel off." She keyed quickly then gestured to the screen. "Like those."

There were skulls, daggers, snarling animals, monsters... "Don't you have anything less gruesome?"

She keyed again. "Like that?"

Hello Kitty, Tweety, Barbie and Ken filled the screen. "For a woman. Someone over twelve."

"Gotcha."

Butterflies and flowers came up. "Those are nice. Let's do them. When do we leave? I don't have time for

Amazon to deliver this stuff. Can one of you conjure it up or should I ask MJ for a wish?"

Becca stopped rocking. "Just what we need, more problems."

Zoe bumped Ursula's arm. "Whatever you do, don't ask Becca for a spell. You may never get out of here, at least sound and sane."

"I heard that." Becca pointed. "I'm getting better at magic, but I want no part of this. Get the stuff from MJ. Zoe, stay with Ursula down there until she's ready to come back up. Do not lose or corrupt her."

"I'd say she's doing a fine job on her own and it'd be better if the guys take her to Farron."

"What?" Ursula and Becca had spoken at the same time.

"Hear me out. They have more clout with the other demons than I do and I've never been to Farron's penthouse. It's my guess security's tight. The guys will have a better chance of getting past that than I would."

Ursula gripped the desk to keep standing. "You mean Taro, Stefin and Anatol will see me dressed, or rather undressed, in those leather things?"

"So will tons of other demons, most of them worse than Farron. Better get over it if you intend to chase after him."

Zoe made her sound foolish. Maybe she was, but she also had feelings. "Must be nice to have guys fall into your lap like yours did then stick around rather than taking off without a word or even a goodbye kiss. I'm not that lucky. This is my only chance at happiness. Don't make fun of me."

"What? I'm not. I wasn't." She hugged her. "Even if it's the wrong thing to do and this can't possibly work out, I'll make sure my guys get you in to see Farron."

Despite Zoe's depressing assessment, Ursula's hope skyrocketed again.

To her surprise, MJ delivered the items as Ursula had wished and stuck around to see how they'd look on her. Heather, Constance and Wynona trickled in for the show.

"Wow." Heather stroked the orgasmic belt. "This is amazing."

MJ bumped her arm. "When we're through here, look in your bottom desk drawer. Got two of those babies. One for you and one for me. For breaks and lunch periods."

They giggled.

"Wait. We need one of these, too." Zoe showed MJ the long black cape Ursula had pointed out earlier.

Ursula didn't understand. "I thought you said it wouldn't do any good at the frisking gate or with Farron's security."

"Maybe we can change that. MJ, do your thing."

A pop rang out. The cape hung over a chair, the garment nicer than the screen version. This one had dainty ruffles on the edges.

Ursula welled up with gratitude and shrank at what was next. "Time for me to get dressed — or rather undressed, huh?"

Zoe hurried to Becca's desk. "Let me get the guys first."

"No. Please. I don't want them watching."

"They won't. I need to have a word with them." She pressed the intercom.

"Stefin here."

"Get your butt, along with Taro's and Anatol's, in Becca's office, pronto."

"We did not break that were's arm. Heather healed it right away."

"Whatever. Just get in here with the others."

They arrived, Stefin in the lead. He hauled Zoe into his arms, his hand on her ass. "Ready for some fun, huh?"

She pushed him into Taro and Anatol. "Listen up." She told them the plan. "Use your clout so Ursula doesn't get frisked at the gate or at Farron's place."

Stefin frowned. "Not even by Farron?"

"By the guards. The only one who sees her naked is Farron, got it?"

Ursula hugged her. "Thanks."

"You bet." She focused on the guys. "Keep her safe. Don't leave her alone for a second."

"Not even with Farron?"

Zoe smacked Stefin's belly. "Quit playing with me."

"Sure you want that?"

They giggled worse than Heather or MJ had and shared an impassioned kiss. Anatol and Taro got in on the action. Entwined, the four demons teetered to the right then left with their unruly lust.

Once they made it past the jamb, Wynona slammed the door on them, threw the lock and faced Ursula. "Show time. Sure you want to do this?"

No. But she had to see Farron again and win him over, or at least get an explanation as to why he was avoiding her. As everyone here already said, the answer might not be good, but at least she wouldn't be drowning in doubt. Crushing sorrow would take its place.

She wilted. "Yeah, I can't wait."

Constance scooted up on the sofa. "Want us to close our eyes until you have on the cape?"

"Or would you like us to leave?" Heather's lovely features brimmed with sympathy. Of course, she was like that with everyone, even the UPS guy when he hauled slightly heavy packages to their door.

Ursula faced the group. "You guys can stay on one condition. Don't say anything mean about Farron." Someone had to protect him. For herself, she had to be strong. No one had to tell her she wasn't beautiful, her bod too curvy, her personality blah. She was well aware of her deficiencies but didn't care about them as long as Farron found her irresistible.

Everyone looked sheepish but nodded. Quiet settled over the group.

Zoe and the guys' lusty makeout session was still going strong in the hall, her breathless moans and their bawdy grunts drowning out everything else.

Wynona slammed her fist against the door.

They quieted.

Ursula figured the worst would be removing her five layers of clothing, not including her knee-high stockings. How wrong she was. No matter how hard she tried, she couldn't figure out the buckles, zippers and locks on the leather stuff.

Wynona and Constance ended up dressing her and pasting on the tats. Oddly enough, Heather offered to help Ursula with the orgasmic belt dildo.

"Thanks, but I think I can handle it myself." Once she had the dildo positioned on her clit, she shifted her weight. The thing buzzed. Tingles shot from her cleft to her eyeballs. She gripped Constance's shoulder.

"You okay?"

Only Farron had turned her on more than the belt did. Even the aversion therapy machine hadn't worked as well. This was freaking great. "Fine."

Wynona handed her a black mask Ursula hadn't seen with the other stuff. Made of satin, lace, feathers and pearls, the thing was far more elegant than the leather gear. "Am I supposed to wear this, too?"

"It might make you feel less exposed."

How true. Once she had it on, she relaxed.

Becca helped her with the cape, securing the jeweled clasp in front. "Be careful, you hear?"

"I'll try." She couldn't promise. Not if it meant she didn't accomplish her goal. She hugged Becca and the others. Each step made her vibrator hum and her world sing. Opting for prudence rather than pleasure, she switched the thing off.

MJ opened the door. Zoe and the guys leaned against the opposite wall, hair mussed, eyes flaming, shirttails pulled out.

Stefin approached first and offered Ursula his arm like a medieval knight.

Pushing aside her doubt and fear of failing, she accepted his grand offer.

Chapter Nine

The guys flanked Ursula and escorted her toward Constance's office. The ladies followed.

Ursula held back. "Shouldn't we be going down rather than horizontal?"

Stefin patted her arm. "In time. We have to get to the right portal first, since you're a good angel."

Already her background was making this complicated. She hoped it wouldn't gum up the works entirely.

In the business end of this place vamps hissed, zombies groaned, weres howled. Staffers barked orders in response. Kenny G's greatest hits filled Constance's shadowed, sensuous office. Candlelight winked off beaded curtains, creating bright colors that danced on the ceiling and walls. Wispy smoke curled from numerous incense sticks in wonderful fragrances — cherry, vanilla, jasmine, even a donut scent. As Martha Stewart often said, 'a good thing'. The pleasant aromas were welcome since the guys' sulfur odor made breathing difficult.

At the jamb, the ladies held back. Each waved bye-bye. Zoe closed the door.

The room plummeted.

Gasping, Ursula gripped Stefin, her legs spread wide to keep her balance. With the descent, everyone's hair flew up.

"Hot damn." Taro pumped his fist. "Way better than El Toro. Six Flags kicks serious ass, but this is one hardcore ride. Amirite?"

The guys whistled and stomped in approval.

Ursula clenched her teeth to keep from shrieking, her cheeks pulled upward by the crazy speed. The walls and floor glowed red. With each passing second, the heat intensified.

Anatol flung out his arms, eyes wild with ecstasy, dreadlocks pointed up. "Wait for it."

She cringed.

The room zoomed down at an insane speed then came to a gentle, bobbing stop. The guys laughed and high-fived each other.

She gagged at the stuffy air, thick with brimstone. On its own, the door flung open. A crimson-and-black world greeted them, the silence so profound it hurt.

The moment they stepped outside the room-elevator, unholy wails sounded in the distance. She flinched.

"Easy." Stefin yanked her hand from him. Her nails had ripped holes in his sleeve.

"Sorry."

"No prob." The ragged tears were already gone, repaired by his dark powers.

Jagged mountains surrounded them, the sky dense with smoke. Smoldering rocks burst into flame. Lava poured from some. The red-gold liquid snaked across the landscape and turned black.

The stuff crunched beneath her boots, but oddly enough didn't melt her soles. Blistering winds roared past, tugging at their hair and clothes. Ursula held her cape tightly to her near nudity. Gloom made it impossible to see too far. Thankfully, an odd golden light lit the way.

She turned her face to the left. The beams followed, pointing straight in front, like headlights on a car. She stopped. "Are my eyes doing that? Glowing?"

Stefin looked. "Yep."

She wasn't certain whether to be grateful or appalled by her newfound skill, since it allowed her to see this place. No wonder Farron came to earth periodically. Here sucked. Unless… "Is what we're seeing real or an illusion to keep undesirables out? Self-righteous turds and fanatics, especially."

Stefin kicked a rock. It rolled away and burst into flame. "The brimstone and fire is real. That, however, is probably a prop." He pointed.

Something resembling a pterodactyl broke through the smoke and dive-bombed at them. She ducked, arm over her head. The thing screeched, rattling her bones, then flew past and snatched a creepy-crawly. It cried out. "No, no, no!"

She shuddered. "I thought that was a huge spider on the ground, not a being that could speak."

Stefin tugged her forward. "Nope."

"Was it real?"

He looked over.

She choked at what looked like bloodstains where the thing had been. "Please tell me this gets better."

"The clubs rule. Here we are."

He and the others stopped at the end of a line that hadn't been there a second before. Countless individuals waited to go through a gargantuan gate, possibly a hundred stories high. Fashioned from black iron, the thing resembled a monster's open mouth. Fangs hung from the top gum. On the ground, skulls and pitted gravestones bordered the walk where the crowd stood.

Magic Kingdom this wasn't.

Spotlights showed where the guards were. She squeezed Stefin's arm and leaned in so the other people, demons, souls, ghouls or whatever they were, couldn't overhear. "Will the guards ask me anything?"

"Name, weight and the crime you committed."

"Why weight?" Revealing that was as bad as being frisked.

"They don't want to overload the boats that take us inland."

Past the gate, several vessels bobbed on oily water. Black skins rather than cloth served as sails.

Stefin bent his head to her. "When they ask your name, it's Elvira. You were damned for near nudity and glorifying gore."

Strangely, that scenario sounded like an old cable show hosted by an actress named Elvira. The slasher flicks she played were awful, her costume shocking, jokes lame. He couldn't mean her. "Do I also fudge on my weight?"

"Up to you, but don't go too far or they'll weigh you in front of everyone and blare the results from the loudspeakers."

No wonder they called this Hell. "They won't touch me, though, right?"

"We'll do our best. Get ready."

They were suddenly first in line.

Two thugs who could have starred in *Conan the Barbarian* blocked them from the gate and boat ramp, their brawny arms, thick necks and sinewy thighs covered in obscene tats depicting nude women and cavorting couples. Neither demon wore clothes, their junk hanging out. Stefin's was too, along with Anatol and Taro's, their work outfits gone, replaced by tights with gaping holes in front to expose their genitals. Whips and riding crops dangled from their wide belts. They'd also donned red capes, which they'd tossed casually over their shoulders. Combat boots rounded out the ensembles. All of them were aroused, cocks rigid, balls plump.

Blushing hotly, Ursula lifted her face.

The thugs drooled at her and winked.

Someone pushed her aside.

"Stefin here." He slammed his fist into his heavily tattooed chest. "Two-hundred-and-twenty pounds. You don't want to know what I've done. It'd make you cry like little girls."

One guard sniffed. The other growled. They went at Stefin. He did the same with them, all pretending to box though no one touched. At last they laughed.

Stefin slung his arms around their necks and shook them soundly. "Boris, Viktor. Is it really you guys beneath that disgusting ink?"

Boris, on the right, gave Stefin the finger. Viktor squirmed, trying to get free. "We know what the ladies want."

All eyes were again on her, the spotlights, too. She squinted and warned herself not to bolt.

Stefin released them and inclined his head to her. "Meet Lolita. Lolita, say hello."

What had happened to Elvira? Without a script, Ursula had no choice except to improvise. "Screw you." If these goons kept her from the boat and Farron, she'd burn them to dust with her glowing irises.

Viktor and Boris shaded their eyes from the glare. Boris spoke to Stefin. "Feisty one, isn't she?"

"Until my friends and I tame her." He stroked his riding crop.

Taro and Anatol did the same with theirs.

"Wouldn't want to keep you guys from it." Boris stepped aside. "Have a nice trip."

As she passed, Viktor smacked her butt.

She started and whirled around.

"Easy, Hagatha." Stefin grabbed Ursula's wrist and hurried her to the boat, Anatol and Taro followed close behind.

She kept her voice low. "I thought it was Elvira."

"Seriously?" He craned his neck. "She's here? Where? I didn't know she'd died. What a shame. Love her show."

This was a nightmare.

Behind them, metal clanked down, the ground shaking with the noise.

The gate had closed, the fangs so closely spaced not even Twiggy, in her heyday, could have slipped past. Spotlights shone on a conservative couple, him in a suit and tie, her in a matronly dress. The style Ursula once preferred before she'd hooked up with Farron.

The couple pushed pamphlets at Viktor and Boris. They reared back.

The woman followed and crowded them. "Listen to me, the time is nigh." Her shrieking voice was worse than nails dragged down a blackboard. "Don't you want to mend your awful ways?"

"Lady, stay away from me." Boris hid behind Viktor.

Her partner shoved pamphlets at him. "With our guidance, you can find a new day. One without lust, gluttony, greed, sloth, wrath, envy and pride."

Boris punched the guy's hand away. "Where's the fucking fun in that?"

"We can help you!"

Guards ran up and dragged the blustery couple away.

The boat was larger than she'd imagined, demons packed shoulder to shoulder. The vessel pitched, rolled and yawed over the now turbulent sea.

She hung on to Anatol's dreadlocks to steady herself. "Am I causing this?" Did the water know she was a good angel?

He pressed his mouth to her ear. "Naw. This is part of the fun."

The others had their arms up and screeched as they would on a rollercoaster. Twice the vessel somersaulted. Water sprayed everyone and dried quickly.

Without warning, she and the guys were off the boat and on land, this area identical to the one they'd left. No buildings. No demons or creatures, either. The crowd they'd been with had vanished. She turned a slow circle but had no idea where everyone had gone, unless they'd sunk beneath the surface.

"Here we go." Taro held open the door of a yellow cab that appeared from nowhere.

She piled in the back seat and adjusted herself so the vibrator wasn't crushing her clit. Taro and Anatol climbed in next. Stefin sat in front next to the skeletal driver who resembled a reaper.

He turned on his meter. "Where to?"

"Tropic of Pleasure."

She tapped Stefin's shoulder. "Is that where Farron lives?"

He squinted at her beaming eyes. "That's what it says here." He showed her his smartphone.

The Hades Guide, similar to Google, displayed Farron's address. It matched the club's. His phone number and email were the same ones she'd used but received no answer. Her stomach rolled. For the first time, she considered he might refuse to see her and would order guards to drag her away as the demons at the gate had with the pushy couple. No one wanted to be told how to feel, nor did they like being blindsided by someone they'd tried to avoid.

Torn between desire and uncertainty, she didn't know what to do.

The cab screeched to a stop.

She hadn't noticed it moving.

The driver pushed out his hand. "Six thousand bucks."

Stefin tossed him a twenty. "Keep the change."

Tropic of Pleasure rose like a monolith from the craggy ground and mountainside, its shape decidedly phallic, the black marble façade glossy in the persistent dusk. The only windows were on the top floor. White lights shone brightly inside as they had in the villa. Because Farron had wanted to see her.

Despite the wonderful memories and stifling heat, she shivered, worried he might have a woman up there and was exploring her nudity in the intense light.

"Sweet." Taro tilted his face to take in the structure that had five hundred stories, according to the Hades Guide. "I had no idea it was this huge."

She didn't understand. "Haven't you guys been here before?"

"We're plebs." Stefin rolled his eyes. "Only the elite go to Farron's joints."

"Are you saying we need an invite?"

"Nope. Brass balls."

He and the guys stormed the front door, pulling her with them.

Demons packed the lobby, the women wearing capes as Ursula did. Some donned masks. The men sported tuxedoes. Their conversations quieted. One after the other looked over.

This was worse than her Vestal Virgin trial. Then, she'd had naïve hope something would spare her. Now, she was a full-blown cynic. Fearing the guys' Domwear had marked them as plebs, she gripped Stefin's arm, or rather, his sleeve. He and the guys wore tuxes now. They escorted her through the crowd with the same confidence royalty or scam artists would use. Equally important, they looked like they belonged here.

Chandeliers in the dozens rained light on the sumptuous surroundings. Fort Knox didn't own this much gold, the precious metal gilding picture frames, furniture and railings. White antique tables mingled with ebony and cherry, the décor exquisitely arranged. Gold brocade and raw silk in sapphire and black graced the sofas and chairs. The floor was blue marble, the cathedral ceiling dotted with lights resembling stars.

The guys led her to a bank of elevators, the white wood doors carved with pornographic images. She should have looked away but didn't. If tonight worked out, she could try out those positions with Farron. Somehow, her vibrator switched itself on and hummed merrily, making her tremble. As discreetly as she could, Ursula turned the stupid thing off, and stopped next to the guys at the last doors.

A demon hulked there, dressed in a metal jockstrap and combat boots, his neck as thick as her thigh, which wasn't dainty. "This one's private for the penthouse."

Stefin slung his arm around her. "We brought Farron a gift. Meet Medea." He chucked her chin.

Flames danced in the hulk's dark eyes, his attention fixed on her cape. "You have weapons under that?"

Only her womanly charms that had always failed her and the dildo that had a mind of its own. "No."

"Love your eyes."

She batted her lashes seductively.

He brought a walkie-talkie to his lips. "Hey, boss. Visitors. One you're gonna want to see." He blew Ursula a kiss.

She caught it.

Farron didn't answer.

Mr. Hulk held up his finger to her and the guys. "Farron, you there?" Static crackled in answer. "You in the can?" More crinkling noises. "Are you with a lady or maybe a group of them?"

Her spirits sank. She didn't want to hear this but couldn't leave. Even if it shattered her, she had to see him one last time and confess her love.

After Hulk had asked about Farron being in the closets, kitchen, pool, exercise and video rooms and received no answer, he shrugged. "Not home."

"What about his office?" Zoe had warned her against cornering Farron there, but Ursula had no choice.

"Let me get on that channel and see." He fiddled with the device then spoke into it. "Hey, Gigi, Drave here. Is boss-man there?"

"Drave? Where are you? I can't see you."

"On my walkie-talkie, doll. See the rectangular black thing on your desk?"

"Wait. Yeah. Your voice is coming from there? How come it's working now but I can't get it to play music?"

"It's not an iPod, babe." He lifted his hairy eyebrows at Ursula and the guys. "Ah, is Farron there?"

"Let me check. Farron!" Silence mingled with static. "Nope, not here. Want me to check the monitors?"

"Please. You're a gem."

Clicking noises sounded over the walkie-talkie. She was either drumming her nails or tap dancing. "Got a hit. He's in the ground-floor bar. Want me to page him?"

Ursula grabbed Drave's device and spoke into it. "No."

She didn't want to give Farron advance warning.

Gigi sighed loudly. "You're my hero. I'm having trouble with the pager — nothing here works right — and he doesn't look too great. Best not to disturb him."

That didn't sound good. "What do you mean?"

"By what? Hey, what happened to your voice? Sounds weird. Like too high and kind of annoying. This thing really isn't working right."

Ursula shoved the device into Drave's burly chest. "Where's the bar?"

He pointed.

She grasped her cape close to cover her near nudity and tore through the crowd. Her ankles wavered from her spike heels. The vibrator whirred again. Dumb thing. Concern, not arousal, pumped through her. Farron couldn't be ill. Demons didn't get sick, as far as she knew. Maybe he'd had a bad day. Working with an admin as clueless as Gigi would do that to a saint.

Ursula skidded to a stop at a wide entrance, the dim room inside moderately busy, couples at the circular bronze tables. Solitary patrons claimed stools at the bar. She forced herself to check the couples first and breathed more easily. Farron wasn't with those women.

The men on stools had their backs to her. Smoky mirrors veined with gold lined the walls. The one behind the bar showed a guy with white hair and silver irises. He caught her reflection and lifted his drink in greeting. The one two stools over wasn't tall or hot enough to be Farron.

Farron slouched on the last stool, surrounded by emptiness, completely alone. Sad for him but delighted for herself, she used her eye beams to traverse the murky space lit only by single black candles on each table. At her approach, patrons glanced up and squinted or frowned at her glowing eyes.

Farron threw back his head and downed whatever was in his shot glass. She would've bet it wasn't ginger ale. His shoulders slumped. Hair hung over his forehead. He rapped the bar.

The female barkeep filled his glass. Her features morphed from Angelina Jolie's to Penelope Cruz, Megan Fox, JLo then back to Angie. She wore a black leather collar, nipple rings and nothing else, at least above her waist. The bar kept Ursula from seeing below it. Farron had a stellar view, but he wasn't looking at skin.

He lifted his glass. It stalled halfway to his mouth. He stared at Ursula's reflection. No, he squinted then shook his head and scrunched his eyes.

Remembering her mask, she whipped it off and hoped he'd recognize her now, despite his alcohol-soaked brain.

His mouth sagged open.

She dashed to him.

He staggered to her.

They met halfway, arms wrapped around each other, mouths joined. He tasted like licorice, herbs and a magnificent demon. She worked her fingers through his hair and held firm to keep him to her. He cupped her ass and yanked her into his ginormous erection. Her dildo powered on at its highest speed. Mega-freaking nice. In their desperate attempt to get closer, they bumped stools, tables and chairs. One fell over and slid across the floor.

Scuffling noises broke out. Patrons skittered away to give them room.

She'd adore them forever for being considerate. This moment belonged to her and Farron. His mouth was hotter than lava, his taste ambrosia, his scent more welcomed than a spring breeze, but better smelling, speaking of passion, immortality, sex, love.

She drew his tongue in more deeply and felt his smile against her lips. He *had* missed her. They made hungry noises that drowned out clinking glasses and whispered conversations. Even Whitney's recording *I Will Always Love You* couldn't compete with the sounds they made. She warbled. Ursula trembled from him and the vibrator.

Farron groaned, pulled free and danced back.

She followed.

He ran into a table. "Ursula?" His eyes nearly popped out. The look a man wears when he's genuinely shocked.

That didn't set well. Who the hell did he think he'd kissed? "Stay still."

He stumbled back. The mirrored wall stopped him.

Discreetly, she turned off the dildo, cupped his face and searched his eyes. The whites were bloodshot, the flames sputtering as if they might go out. She wasn't certain that was possible for a demon. It might be tantamount to a mortal having a heart attack. Only in his case he wouldn't die, he might simply evaporate and not be able to congeal again. "How much did you drink?"

"Ursula?"

"No." Stefin was suddenly beside her. "That's Griselda."

Anatol and Taro joined them.

She glared at Stefin. "You can drop the act. Farron knows who I am."

"No one else here does."

She didn't care about them. "Do you mind? I'd like to talk to him without you guys around."

"Zoe said we shouldn't leave you alone for a second."

"With strangers."

"She didn't specify. No way am I pissing her off. Right, men?" Taro and Anatol nodded. Stefin pointed at the bar. "We'll wait there."

With her chaperones occupied, she concentrated on Farron.

He shielded his eyes from her golden gaze. "What are you doing here?"

"Looking for you."

He brightened then frowned. "Why?"

He couldn't be serious. "You left so suddenly. My calls went to voicemail. You didn't answer my email, mainly because your account's been closed. As far as the texts I sent, you didn't answer one. I would've done more, but I didn't know what to say. You never told me when we were getting together for our next date. We had an awesome time on our first one. It was magic, literally and figuratively. I want to do that again. Wherever you want to go."

He clutched his head. "How'd you get past the gate down here? You're a goo—you shouldn't have. Why are you dressed like that?" He yanked her cape open, gaped, smiled then shut the thing. "Is that an orgasmic belt?"

The vibrator started again. She sagged into him, pussy congested, heat bursting then flooding her with striking warmth. "Oh, yeah."

"Stop it. Now."

"I've tried. It keeps coming on by itself. Must be defective. I can take off the belt. Did you want to play with me?"

"What? No. Quit acting like this."

Her euphoric haze lifted, leaving her sickened. "What?"

He eased her off him, his gaze stone-cold sober, frown deep. "What in the fuck do you think you're doing here?" Despite his harsh tone, he spoke quietly. "You don't belong in a place like this."

"I belong with you, wherever you are."

His glare softened then hardened again. He looked at the bar. "Stefin, get your ass over here."

"Why are you calling him?"

"To take you home."

This couldn't be the end. She refused to believe it. "My home is with you."

He gritted his teeth. "Stop saying that."

"No. Not until you tell me why you left so suddenly the other day without any explanation."

"Our date was over. I had no reason to stay."

She was the reason. Ursula pressed her fists to her chest. "You can't mean that."

"Why not? It was a simple, freaking date. A one-time deal, that's it."

"Since when? You never said that while we were together."

"You didn't give me a chance. I'm saying it now. We had our date. It's over."

"Why?"

He threw up his hands. "You want more explanations?"

"How about the truth on why you were hot for me but then you got cold? During our date, you weren't drunk and suddenly sober, so that doesn't explain it. Becca didn't call ordering you to stay away from me. I know because I asked. Something inside you must have changed. Fine. Tell me what it is. Say you hate me, say you can't stand the sight of my face, that touching me makes you want to hurl and you wish I was dead."

He bounced in place, his face reddened. "Angels. Can't. Die."

"Big frigging deal. Say the words—more importantly, make me believe them—and I'll leave." She stepped back and crossed her arms. "Go on. I'm waiting."

Farron bared his teeth. "Stefin!"

She pointed at him. "Stay where you are."

He hadn't budged, a vodka bottle in his hand, chin lifted. "Neither of you owns me. I only take orders from Zoe."

Farron swore beneath his breath.

Ursula leaned closer and cupped her ear. "What was that? I didn't get it."

"I don't want you here or around me ever again. Didn't I make myself clear when I left you in the treatment room and couldn't get away fast enough? Do I need to paint a fucking picture?"

Pain more horrible than any she'd known sliced through her. Not from his words, his tone. Frustrated. Cruel. Cold. That was the worst. She could accept anything except his indifference or his lies. "You painted me one when you raced across this room the moment you saw me. You did it with your kiss and your embrace. What was that about? Do you greet all women that way?"

"As a matter of fact, I do. Remember how I was on Heather the first day you and I met?"

"If I'm around a zillion more centuries, I'll never forget anything about you. Good or bad, I accept it all."

His frown faded. He glanced to the side, pain on his face. "Why are you making this so pissing hard?"

"Because that day with Heather wasn't you. Right here, right now is." Tears rolled down her cheeks. "When you saw me a moment ago, you wanted me. Don't deny it. I won't believe you."

He bunched his shoulders. "You're seeing what you want to. Not what's real. Are you going to force me to throw you out?"

"I have every right to be here, just as you do."

"What are you talking about? I own the damn place."

"I'm a patron. If you don't want to play with me, I'll find a demon who will." She ripped off the clasp holding her cape together and tossed the garment aside.

Chair legs scraped behind them. Mirrors reflected male and female demons who'd turned to look. The guys spied her naked ass and tats, the ladies her thighs, each assessing the goods.

Ursula refused to cringe. So, she wasn't built like Kate Moss. Who was without Photoshop? This was who she was. A good angel who wasn't going to let men dump her any longer or allow them to set the rules. Her time had come. Better get used to it.

She stormed off to show she wasn't a pushover any longer.

Farron caught her wrist.

Thrilled, she looked over, ready to jump in his arms. "I knew you'd change your mind."

"I haven't. I want you out of here."

A slap couldn't have hurt her more. "Fine. I'm leaving your precious bar. I want to check out the club, anyway."

"Not a chance."

"Wanna bet?" She clawed him.

"Shit." He released her.

She stomped away.

He caught up. "Don't make me spank you."

She whirled on him, aroused and pissed, an exciting combination. She shook off her desire. "Never again, mister. You and I are through, remember? I'm going to have fun with a real demon. Maybe S himself."

Farron hauled her over his shoulder.

She wilted against him and cupped his ass. "Are we going to your penthouse?"

"You're going home if I have to UPS you there."

She pummeled his back. "Let go of me."

"Once we're outside and you're on your way home."

"Guys! Help! Now!"

They turned on their stools, drinks in hand. Taro finished his beer. "Not until he takes you out of our sight."

"Stop him right this freaking minute or I'm telling Zoe on you."

They were on her and Farron in a New York minute, pulling her away and pinning him to the mirrored wall with their powers.

She slapped Anatol's arm. "Don't hurt him."

"Make up your mind."

"Keep him here, uninjured, got it?"

Farron fought like a maniac, chest heaving, fists clenched. "Ursula!"

She ignored his shout and ran from the bar.

Chapter Ten

Stuck fast to the wall, Farron bellowed. His roar shook the room. Mirrors cracked and patrons dove beneath tables. The barkeep caught bottles falling from shelves.

Stefin sauntered to his stool. Anatol gripped his arm and stopped him from sitting. "Shouldn't we follow Ursula?"

"If we leave here, who's going to keep Farron from going after her?"

Taro rocked on his heels. "Looks like we have ourselves a Mexican standoff."

They regained their stools and knocked back their drinks.

Farron seethed at them. Each a moron, Stefin the worse. How dare they give him a hard time. They couldn't actually think their puny powers would stop him. He lifted his head. "Drave!"

With his howl, chairs jumped, candlelight flickered and his security chief tore into the room.

Farron glared. The nitwit should have policed the monitors and seen the mess going on in here. Gigi should have done so, too. Her, Farron could forgive for not doing anything to help. She had nice boobs. Drave? He was an ugly SOB. "Get. Me. Down."

"Yes, sir."

With one hand, Drave shot fireballs at the three stooges. They did the same to him so he couldn't release Farron. Drave parried the volleys and hollered into his walkie-talkie for backup.

Security poured into the bar dressed in riot gear — impenetrable facemasks, titanium jockstraps, like Drave's, to protect a man's junk from ricocheting power and combat boots because the shoes looked cool. Other than that, the guys were naked.

The battle escalated. Light flashed brighter than a thousand exploding suns. Sonic booms rattled the space and Farron's teeth. He growled louder than the other sounds.

Everything fell quiet except for Whitney's recording, *Saving All My Love for You*.

Smoke cleared. The barkeep sprawled on the counter, a vamp with silver eyes on top of her. He sucked her throat. She'd planted her hands on his head, keeping him close. Patrons righted their tables and chairs, took a load off and resumed drinking. Anatol, Stefin and Taro hung from the ceiling in gold cages.

Stefin stuck his hand through the bars. "My vodka."

"Not in a zillion years." Freed, Farron pushed off the floor. "Lilith." His barkeep. "No more drinks for him or the other caged goons, got it?"

With her eyes closed and her mouth welded to the vamp's, she gave Farron a thumbs-up.

Stefin huffed. "I paid for that."

"Screw you." Farron tore from the bar to find Ursula before she got hurt or had a good time with someone other than him.

He'd vaporize anyone who dared touch her. She was his, damn it.

His step faltered. She didn't belong to him. A truth he had to remember and believe. She was a good angel. He was vermin. Why the fuck did she have to come here and screw with his head again?

She'd looked fantastic. Her nipples, boobs, furry mound, that outstanding orgasmic belt, slave harness and those tats. Wow. She could have been a model for those online fetish sites, looking sweetly sinful. The best of both worlds. Yet nothing could compare with her gold eyes. They'd beamed more brightly on him than anyone else. Arousal and tenderness had shone on her gorgeous features.

He ached from too much desire. Love that couldn't happen. Why didn't she understand how doomed they were, be a good girl and wing back to Heaven, leaving him to a future spent in bars, knocking back absinthe?

Farron raced through the lobby. She wasn't anywhere here, which wasn't possible. She was one in a gazillion, which meant he couldn't have missed her. She also had no way to reach the fetish rooms unless she had a map. Staff offered those and detailed directions at the front desk.

He slammed his fist on the counter. Two male demons and one female named Spice, hustled over, naked except for their slave collars and biceps bracelets with the company logo emblazoned on them. The club's standard uniform.

"Yes, sir." They'd spoken as one.

"I'm looking for a woman."

They pointed behind him to the numerous females in the crowd.

"Not them." They'd never compare to Ursula. "She's about five-five without heels, with them she comes to here on me." He pointed at his chin. "She has soft brown hair that falls in fabulous waves to her shoulders. Her locks are unbelievably soft, like her cheeks. Those babies have a faint rose tint, matching her mouth and nip—never mind that. She has a mole on her right boo—ah, she has two tats on her back and was wearing a slave harness, orgasmic belt and extreme boots. She might be walking funny, not because of the boots, the belt. The dil—attachment keeps turning on by itself. Her eyes are pure gold and shining, like headlights. Where'd she go?"

They lifted their shoulders as one.

He gripped the counter, breaking off handfuls of granite. "You must have seen her when she asked for a map."

Spice shook her head. "No one looking like that asked for one."

Ursula couldn't have taken an elevator to another floor. Only a demon's thumbprint and DNA on the buttons operated the lifts. A security precaution to keep zealots from handing out pamphlets and bothering the clientele. Farron tossed the granite aside and pointed at Spice. "Check the ladies' room."

He didn't think Ursula would have wandered into the men's room, but who knew? Her eyes might be giving her problems. He ordered the male staff to check there then sprinted outside, hoping he'd see her, worried if he did he'd have to be a louse again so she'd leave for good. Being mean to her killed him. However, ruining her future with his presence and selfish love wasn't something he could do.

A lone yellow cab had parked outside. Howling winds rocked it. A butt-ugly reaper leaned against the tottering vehicle.

Farron shouted above the gale. "Did you see a woman out here with beaming yellow eyes? Did you give her a ride back to Earth?"

She had to be safe, finally. That was the only thing he had a right to ask for.

The reaper put out his hand. "Two million bucks and I talk."

Farron's dark powers surged before he could contain them. He tossed the reaper around like a rag doll, shot him to the next universe then dragged him back to this one and the depths of Hell.

The hideous fart curled in a ball on the cab roof. "I brought her here with three demons. Haven't seen her since, I swear."

Farron swore, pivoted and fought the wind to get back inside.

"Hey, don't I get a tip for the info?"

He tossed him a hundred dollar bill. The reaper jumped, but missed. A gust pulled the money away.

Inside, Farron nearly collided with Spice. He reared back.

She did, too. "She wasn't in the ladies' room."

The male staff left the men's room and shook their heads.

An icy chill ran down Farron's spine. What little he'd eaten these last days threatened to come up. If Ursula wasn't down here, she had to be on an overhead floor, escorted there by a demon with lust on his mind. More than four hundred rooms, some private, others for group activities, would give him a chance to do whatever he willed to her.

Prick. Bastard. Dead man. The fool would learn what screwing around with Farron's woman meant.

His knees buckled. She wasn't his woman. Never would be.

Determined to remember that, he hollered for security and the desk staff. They gathered around.

He described Ursula again. "I need to find her. Check the monitors in every room, private and group. Do the same with those in the halls. Question the guests down here."

The patrons laughed and chatted, paying no attention to the ruckus, a normal occurrence since plebs or proselytizers were always trying to sneak in.

"Drave." Farron pointed. "I want to see the lobby security tapes. Roll them back to a half hour ago. Bring them to the front desk. All of you, *go*."

His staff scattered. He cornered a nearby demon and asked the guy what he'd seen.

* * * *

Ursula finally understood what BDSM really stood for — bad, depraved, sinful and merciless. Or maybe the M was another code word for manacles. There were plenty around. Nasty irons hugged women's wrists and ankles, securing them to tables, posts, X-frames, walls and even chains hanging from the ceiling in the gothic, dungeon-like room. The ladies' toes dangled inches off the stone floor, their faces flushed with desire, mouths opened on keening wails and delighted sobs.

Weird, but oddly arousing.

Doms roamed the room dressed in the same gear Stefin and the guys had donned earlier, except these demons wore hoods that hid everything but their fiery eyes and cruel mouths. A nice menacing touch, like the whips, paddles and crops they carried.

Her pussy twitched for reasons she couldn't imagine since her vibrator hadn't switched on and this scene should have appalled rather than excited her. Her 'date' certainly wasn't thrilling her.

She'd met Hannibal in the lobby. He'd been the only receptive demon there despite her nearly naked state. She'd asked to see the sights. He'd promised to show her. No surprise. Women probably fell at his feet on an hourly basis, especially plain Janes like her, giving him what he wanted most — an adoring audience. His long blond hair was silkier than Heather's, eyes bluer than the lobby floor, muscles and body hair in all the right places, the package between his legs first rate, his sulky good looks marking him as a mega bad boy.

He cupped her ass.

She shoved his hand away for the nth time since they'd met. Like five minutes ago. The ladies at the service had said Farron was bad. They should meet this guy.

He cradled her breast.

She elbowed him.

He growled. "I'm the one who's supposed to punish you."

Yep, she'd caught on fast to BDSM rules. The ladies got paddled, whipped or caned while the guys strutted like masters of the universe, everyone having a grand time. She wanted to join in but not with Hannibal or anyone else here. Only Farron, even though he'd crushed her as no one else had and she'd then pissed him off.

Ursula hoped he hadn't hurt Anatol or the guys too badly when he'd broken free. She'd expected him to be here by now, following her, his jealousy raging, his protectiveness too. Goading him with Hannibal was juvenile, but she didn't know what other steps to take to get Farron to admit his love. Or at least offer to go on another date with her so she could wear him down.

"Whoa." She twisted her wrist to break from Hannibal's grip but couldn't. "What are you doing?"

"Taking charge."

Not with her. "Hey." She dug in her heels.

He dragged her to a post. Her boots dug gouges in the floor. Once there, he clamped manacles on her wrists but left her ankles unfettered. She tugged on the irons. Neither they, nor the chains, gave an inch. Alarmed, she rounded the post to keep away from him.

He pursued, stroking the punishment tools hanging from his belt and tried to get to her ass. She, in turn, was determined to keep her butt from him. They circled the post like an out-of-control merry-go-round.

"Fuck." He covered his mouth. "Chasing you in circles is making me queasy. Keep still."

Not a chance.

His eyes flashed. "To hell with this."

Something sucked at her soles, cementing them to the floor, keeping her from fleeing.

With a masterful smile, he rounded her.

She twisted quickly and yanked on her chains to grab his balls. Success. She squeezed hard enough to crack his nuts.

His face turned white then purple, his eyes flames nearly snuffing out like Farron's had earlier, just before his knees collapsed.

He rocked in a fetal position. Air whooshed from between his lips, but he didn't produce any words. Curses would eventually come.

She leaned down as well as she could, given the restraints. "Sorry."

"Looks like we have a scrappy one here."

Boots clomped on the floor. Two demons with hoods.

Despite Hannibal's current condition, his power kept Ursula's feet fused to the spot, giving her no chance to back away. One, or perhaps both, of these demons had done the same with her hands. She couldn't lift them to protect herself.

Sweating badly, she smiled. "Hi, guys. I'm new at this. Learner's curve, you know. I promise I won't make any more fuss."

The taller demon with the blackest eyes rested his hand on her belly, his fingers perilously close to her mound. "Damn right, you won't. I'll teach you how to behave like a good little sub should."

"*We'll* teach her." The other demon joined them, his eye flames blue like a welding torch. "I want in on the play." He grabbed her butt. "We'll pink up this baby real nice."

Full-blown panic made her extra hot. "Please. You don't understand. Despite my gold eyes, I'm not a—"

Mr. Blue Flames cut off her plea with his mouth soldered to hers. She clenched her teeth before his tongue became a problem. He swatted her butt. No good. Foreplay wasn't going to change her mind about French kissing him. She gritted her teeth even harder.

He flew backward and crashed against the wall. The other guy somersaulted away from her, also backward, and came to rest on an empty table, his husky arms and legs drooped over the sides.

Surely, she hadn't done that with her revulsion or thoughts.

Whistling noises from canes, smacks from paddles and the resulting rapturous cries from subs quieted. Ursula suspected everyone stared at and possibly feared her. Nope. No one seemed to know she existed. The crowd looked at the doorway.

Farron.

Delight played across Ursula's features, followed by caution.

His fault. Farron hated himself for suppressing her innocent charm but had no choice. What the Doms would have done to her would've been far worse, taking what didn't belong to them and she didn't want to give. Terror would have registered in her beautiful eyes.

How dare they do that to his woman?

No, no, no, not his woman, never that. Fuck, when was he going to remember such a simple concept? He tightened his jaw, his patience with himself and the Doms at an end. Fury fueled his power. He flung them from the room as he would soiled rags and tossed Hannibal next. The guy clutched his bruised boys.

The remaining demons didn't speak or seem to breathe. They weren't that brave around him.

Ursula was. She pinned him with her gaze...maybe challenged him as she'd done downstairs.

He crossed the room to her. Torches on the rough stone walls lit his way. Her eyes helped too, the beams cutting through the shadows, shining only on him.

She lifted her face and looked down her nose. "What?"

He really hated that word, probably as much as she had when he'd repeatedly said the same to her the day they'd met. If he'd known then she'd twist him into knots, steal his good sense and replace it with yearning and impossible need, he would have begged Anatol for the free castration.

Too much testosterone whizzed through him now, his fists bunched, throat constricted. "What do you think?"

"If you treat all your patrons as you did my guys in here, you're going to lose business. That's not wise."

"Maybe not. But they're not yours, and you're not a patron."

"Is that what you think?" She laughed and looked over at another demon. "Hey, you, with the ugly horse head tattooed on your chest. Come here."

The guy looked down. "That's a goat's head. The mark of Satan."

"Whatever. Come to mama."

He glanced at Farron. "You mind?"

"Do what she wants and you'll find out."

"Sorry, babe." He held up his hands. "No can do. I got a wife and in-laws at home with more family freeloaders on the way. I only work here. Right?" He looked at Farron hopefully.

She spoke to the others. "Who wants to play with me? Singles only. I'm talking about relationship status, not how many can join in at the same time. I don't want anyone who's engaged or going steady, either. If you're in a friends-with-benefits relationship, that's cool."

Farron put out his hand to keep everyone back and tried to reason with her. "Is that what you want? Screwing around just to be screwing around?"

Something flashed in her eyes that he couldn't read. She pushed it aside and squared her shoulders. "I'm here, aren't I? Quit getting in my way and everyone else's, or do the deed yourself...if you're demon enough."

Gasps broke out.

He ignored them but not her smug look. *Of all the...* He was trying to save her from herself. Hell, he wanted to spare her from him but she wasn't having it, preferring to drive him batshit crazy with lust. How dare she when he was hurting worse than he believed possible. These last days had been more horrible than Hell — missing her like mad, wishing there was a way to make their relationship work. There wasn't. His indignation rose. Walls creaked. Dirt trickled from the widening cracks. Torches erupted. Those flames scorched the ceiling. Several Doms and ladies who weren't chained down fled.

Ursula didn't bat an eye. "Just a suggestion, but you need to work on controlling your power. Some might think you're too emotional, not in charge like a Dom should be. Maybe you don't know how that is. Maybe someone should teach you."

"Maybe you need a damn spanking."

Color stained her cheeks. "That's why I'm here. Searching for a demon who's man enough to do it." She looked at the remaining guys.

Farron brought her face back, claimed her mouth and thrust his tongue inside. She sucked so hard his tongue hurt. He wanted more. How nuts was that in addition to being futile, but the only solution. Exposing her to his depravity might chase her away faster than his pleas ever would. He'd show her what a real Dom did.

His kiss was hard and greedy, demanding she surrender.

She didn't fight him.

Farron wasn't surprised. They hadn't started yet, though they would. He pulled free and snapped his fingers at a Dom near the wall. "Blindfold, gag, strap, now." He put out his hand.

She rubbed her cheek against his arm.

Affection bubbled up. If he could have given her the world, he would have. Sadly, he couldn't come close. That left shoving away his tender feelings and being a motherfucker. He gripped her hair and pulled back her head. "None of that. I'm your master. You're my slave. You don't make a move without my consent."

"Oh, yeah? Prove it."

Refusing to laugh, he swatted her butt. "Quiet or there will be more punishment."

"I haven't had any yet except a few puny smacks."

What a mouth. Too bad he liked her sass. "Remember this moment when you're mine to do with as I will."

"I'm still waiting."

A female demon giggled.

"Hey, you." Ursula glared at the woman. "No making fun. You should be so lucky to have him threatening you with stuff he can't seem to start."

Can't what? Farron unlocked Ursula's manacles and pulled her to a table. A camera mounted on a tripod stood to the side. He switched on the device. Simultaneously, a screen whirred down from the ceiling, providing a perfect view of whatever would happen at the table.

Ursula's cheeks blazed. She wasn't so cocky now. "You make porn here?"

This would be for his private collection, along with the security footage of her. All he'd have left once she was gone. He imagined the images playing on his office walls, driving him nuts and to drink. "Is there a problem?"

She searched his face, uncertainty and arousal mingled on hers. "I'm ready for anything. I told you that days ago. I want you to teach me this stuff. What you like. Show me, please."

He wasn't certain whether to laugh or groan. She'd missed her calling as an admin angel. She should have been a hostage negotiator given her gift for dispelling a man's anger faster than a bullet to his brain. "I don't like this stuff with you."

"You haven't tried. I'm game. Actually, I'm excited."

Her eyes were on high-beam now, proving her words and screwing up his plan. He was supposed to frighten her with this, not send her over the moon. "Others are here."

"Yeah, voyeurism. Like you suggested in Rome. Awesome."

"Screw that." He stepped back. "You're only doing this for me."

"Me, too. I know you're planning to cut out after this. I'm not stupid or even that naïve. I want us to do something mega hot as a kind of keepsake. Stuff I can look back on when you're gone. Can I have a copy of the tape and any pictures of you that you don't mind giving up?"

Sorrow crowded him. If she kept this up, he'd be sobbing like a woman. "Don't talk like that."

"You mean the truth? I can't lie, I'm a goo—"

He slapped his hand over her mouth before she told everyone she was a good angel and didn't belong here, which she didn't. "What did I tell you about talking?"

She licked his palm.

He lowered his face, certain he wouldn't survive this and he only had himself to blame.

Earlier, when Drave had spotted her in this room and gathered the SWAT team to pull her out, Farron had nixed the idea, wanting to rescue her himself. He had to see her again, touch, kiss and love her once more.

They were lying to themselves and each other, but he couldn't stop. After he disciplined her, he'd send in the troops and have them haul her away before he lost his head again.

He removed her orgasmic belt and dildo. Given the heat and plastic stench, the motor had burnt out from overuse.

She sighed. "Thanks, that was getting annoying. I prefer your hands on me."

She was determined to drive him batty.

He secured her wrists to manacles bolted to the tabletop then her ankles to the ones on the table legs. "Bend over."

She did. Far too willingly.

The gag, blindfold and strap he'd demanded earlier lay on the table. Rather than use the silk gag, he guided her to a leather-covered phallus bolted to a stand on the table, the device horizontal with her mouth. Its purpose similar to a ball-gag—to keep a sub quiet during punishment.

Ursula licked and sucked the thing as she had his cock.

Fighting a smile, he stroked her pretty tattoos then pressed the small of her back. "Lift your ass." Thanks to the manacles, she'd already had to spread her legs. "Present yourself."

She gave him no grief.

He repositioned the camera for an unrestricted view of her elevated ass and both openings, her pussy drenched, folds plump and dark pink. Her privacy belonged to him and the others now.

She lifted her face to the screen, her cleft in full view and glorious Technicolor.

He waited for her to cringe, whimper or beg him to stop. No way would he go forward without her full consent.

She gnawed on the phallus then took the thing more deeply into her mouth.

Damn, she was a real trouper. "Ready?"

She nodded.

His clothes disappeared, his cock rigid enough to point at the ceiling, balls firm as unripe tomatoes and as heavy, too. He fingered the supple punishment strap, its smooth leather for BDSM babies, not those who got off on pain.

He couldn't hurt her. Not even if he'd caught her *in flagrante delicto* with Hannibal. Farron would have destroyed himself first to ease his jealousy and pain.

He stroked her ass and almost lost what little restraint he had. Her skin was softer than a petal. The dimples above her cheeks made him smile. Even her rosy ring was beautiful, tightening from his touch. Her cleft and clit filled him with wonder, the kind a man should treasure. No luxury car, fancy penthouse, wealth or power could compete with a woman's gifts, especially if she gave them willingly to a man she trusted and craved.

Ursula shouldn't have done that with him. He didn't deserve it. What's more, he'd warned her away from him, but she wouldn't turn back. Right now, he couldn't either. Later would be a different story, as she'd said. He stroked her cleft. She made a wanting, feminine sound. Powerful music to soothe a demon's loneliness.

Committed to this one last act before they parted forever, he worked her nub to coax her toward climax. Her fingers curled and squeezed. She wiggled her ass but couldn't get away from him. Delighted, he teased her sex relentlessly but wouldn't let her come. Now that he'd trapped, used and viewed her, she had no option except to surrender.

A low moan escaped her lips. She sucked harder on the phallus.

Pity, it wasn't his cock. Frustrated and longing, he stepped back then snapped the belt.

She stilled.

Neither of them breathed. The area in front of her darkened. He suspected she'd closed her eyes. "I won't hurt you." He meant that in every way. "You have nothing to be afraid of."

The beams returned, her eyes opened again. She nodded.

"Ready?"

Another nod. This one wasn't as enthusiastic but she'd still agreed.

He lifted the strap.

The end flew up, momentarily suspended.

Farron brought it down.

The crack sounded worse than he'd wanted. A pink stripe marred her perfect skin.

The crowd erupted in applause.

He gestured them to keep quiet and bent down to her. "Are you okay?"

She edged back to release the phallus from her mouth. "Sure. Don't stop. Do it again."

St. Peter needed to have a talk with her. "You can't be serious."

"Why not? Because of who I am? You should have seen how Wynona turned Rafael around. He's almost as lascivious as you are. Or at least how you used to be."

"You're not going to insult me into doing this."

She glanced past him. "The troops are getting restless."

Feet shuffling, murmurs and several muttered oaths filled the room.

"Fuck 'em. They won't dare cross me. They don't have the balls."

"Not like yours, that's for sure. Those bad boys are in a class all by themselves." Her sauciness turned beatific. "C'mon. Don't make me wait. For anything." She gave him a pleading look then smiled.

He did too. How, he wasn't certain since neither of them would be grinning later. Unwilling to think about their sexual hangover, he shook out the kinks in his shoulders. "Hang on."

"I'm not going anywhere."

That's what he was afraid of. He waited until she'd slid the phallus back into her mouth before he swung the strap and brought it down on her.

The spectators whistled and stomped their feet.

She whimpered then lifted her ass. A sure sign she wanted more.

Farron punished her well. Her butt turned rosy. Each crack produced a delirious cry.

He hoped to hell that was good on her part and not her trying to give him what she thought he wanted so he wouldn't cut out.

Panting, she sagged against the table.

He tossed the strap and mounted her, driving his cock deeply inside, her cunt nothing more than a temporary home, the only one he desired.

She squeezed his rod fast and slow.

His laughter filled the room.

Hers did, too.

With their fingers laced, they held tight to each other.

He pumped and lost himself in her slippery heat, the miracle of simply being with her a little longer.

Chapter Eleven

Ursula enjoyed the ride of her life, not caring what anyone thought. She'd worried about other people's perceptions and feelings far too much during her Vestal Virgin days. In Heaven, she'd made the same mistake, following orders readily and without question, settling for a guy everyone said she should be with even though he wasn't that into her.

Meeting Farron had allowed her to become the woman she was today. Love made everything possible. So did trust and honor. In an environment where a man and a woman explored their desires willingly, shame had no chance to take root, only joy.

She'd missed so much by not knowing the truth until now. Of course, she'd had to wait for him to come along.

His thrusts were a wonder, his shaft invading her depths with unparalleled strength, but also filling her with warmth and desire. She squeezed his fingers. He did the same with hers then pulled his hand free and stroked her nub.

She soared, her wings unnecessary, his touch sending her to a place she adored. Heated. Sensual. Serene. What no drug or alcohol could accomplish. Lovers had the patent on this magic.

He quickened his pumps, his rod monstrous, her sheath engorged. They came together. He bellowed like the demon he was. The vibrant sound widened fissures in the walls and ceiling.

Dust rained on them. She sneezed.

Sweaty and panting, he embraced her. "You all right?"

"I want more." She was a hopeless glutton when it came to him.

Those watching cheered. She'd forgotten about them. They pressed in despite the screen giving them a ringside seat to the action.

Farron growled.

Everyone disappeared.

Ursula blinked then shook her head to clear it. The patrons hadn't left. She and Farron had, the dungeon room gone and replaced by what she guessed was his penthouse. Windowed walls showed a star-splashed sky. A gigantic harvest moon seemed to emerge from an ocean, the water sparkling like a bajillion diamonds and lighting the room better than lamps. "What's outside your windows isn't real, right?"

Abruptly, they were face to face. She didn't recall turning over.

He nuzzled her neck.

Passion claimed her. Clinging to each other, they rolled across a slippery surface, her manacles, slave harness and boots history. She wrapped her legs around his lean hips.

He sucked her throat.

Her skin stung. He was giving her a hickey, marking her as his. Overjoyed, she got them rolling again without running into furniture or a wall. Weird. She opened one eye. They were on a huge circular bed. The red satin sheets smelled like amber, honey and musk. Her fragrance, not his. "What happened to your scent?"

He kissed her neck where he'd just sucked. "Yours smells better."

Not to her. "What happened to the outside?"

He lifted his head and peered at the expansive windows. "Nothing. It's still there."

So was his hickey, though the bruise had faded a bit. She'd have to tend to it later. "Why'd you change the scenery that's normally out there?"

"This is better."

He didn't know how wrong he was. She wanted him as he came, not an image he needed to portray. He'd spent his existence trying to be a bad boy to keep up an act that didn't make him happy. No different from her goody two-shoes performance. That sucked. "What's real is fine. Show me."

Lava spewed on the windows and slithered down the panes, leaving a smoke trail. The black wisps formed menacing clouds. Lightning pulsed within them that brightened the room to silver before the gloom turned blood red again. Okay, even if she didn't need him changed, the outside could use a little finesse. "I'm willing to admit when I'm mistaken." She cupped his head. "But I want your scent back. Now. No arguments or delays."

Sulfur and musk greeted her, along with his endless doubt. Despair flooded his face.

Before he could lecture her on their pointless attraction, she kissed him hungrily. She'd never be wrong about them and would fight for their future. Ardently, she sucked his tongue.

He grunted and revved his engines, his melancholy lifted. The returned moon bathed them in its shimmering glow. A lush instrumental played, combining classical and pop. Two distinct sounds that proved perfect together. If the differing music types fit, he and she could, too.

She pulled her mouth free, slid down, turned and straddled him, her back to his front. "Hungry?" She looked over.

His dimpled smile was worth all the crap life threw at her.

He grabbed her hips, his touch sizzling. "What do you think?"

His cock bumped into her cleft, providing the best possible answer.

Giggling, she scooted down until her pussy hovered above his face and his precious cargo lay beneath hers, his fragrance pure sin. "Don't hold back. Indulge."

Satisfaction was definitely on their itinerary. Tonight was about satisfaction and bonding. There was no need to rush. They had an eternity to be together. She'd accept nothing less. First, she smelled him then nipped at his musky curls.

He did the same with hers and sighed like a weary traveler who'd found peace at last.

She'd comfort him endlessly and would thrill him, too. That was her new job. The only one she wanted.

With his boys cradled in her palm, she took his rod into her mouth.

He sucked air. His belly bumped into her and his balls plumped between her fingers. She couldn't have asked for a better reaction. Hunkered down, she sucked his cock and fondled his nuts.

His breath spilled out, warming her pussy, followed by him licking her clit.

Delight mushroomed too quickly, urging her to come. She didn't want to as yet. Trembling, she pulled up.

He hauled her back down, his viselike grip giving no quarter. She was his to do with as he willed.

Glory hallelujahs rang in her head.

She gorged on him as he did with her, the noises they made brazen but honest and wonderfully irrepressible. He came a tad before she did, the distinction unimportant and certainly not something she'd boast about. Taking care of each other's egos and soothing pain or disappointments had to be their only goal.

Ursula savored his cum as she would the finest wine. Finished, she fell over his leg and gulped air. He scooted off the mattress. She reached for him. "Where are you going?"

"You'll see." He slung her on his shoulder like a sack stuffed with grain.

She wanted to believe this was a good thing but wasn't certain. Anxious, she searched for the front door, fearful the bewitching hour between them had passed, and despite her previous glee, he was going to ditch her. Again.

The door loomed to the right. Farron padded left. The moon followed, lighting their way.

This was too cool. She gripped his butt. "Where are we going?"

"It's a surprise."

Maybe he had a Dom room up here, the ultimate man cave.

Wait. Maybe? Who was she kidding? He was Farron, the baddest demon ever.

His butt cheeks flexed with each step and made her even wetter, the same as his strength. She wasn't built like a stick, yet he carried her as he would a feather, not breaking a sweat. Without trying, he made her feel beautiful and wanted. Happy, she kissed his spine.

His feet slapped marble. Beneath those sounds, something else intruded. Rustling or lapping. The noise surf makes when it licks the shore, or in this case, the windows. Nope. The ocean was no different from before, nonintrusive and completely romantic.

"Here we are." He stopped.

The pool was as long as a football field. Dense steam rose from water, the marble walls blacker than night. A skylight substituted for the ceiling. Stars winked down at them, the harvest moon too, having switched location.

This was better than a romance novel. She squeezed his ass.

He jumped in the pool.

Alarmed, Ursula lost it. "Wait!"

A breath above the water they halted. Chlorine bit her nostrils. She hung onto him for dear life, probably putting dents in his back. "How hot is that?"

Despite her reckless passion and glowing eyes, she was still a good angel. Third-degree burns she didn't need.

He tightened his arm on her. "Tepid for me. Stick your finger in it."

She found the water mild and pleasant. "Nice. Why all the steam?"

"Atmosphere. I thought you'd like it."

He'd done it again, trying to make things perfect when they didn't have to be. She couldn't scold, though—too moved that he'd done this for her. "Thanks. You like Kenny G.?"

"Hell, no."

"Henri Mancini?"

"I can live with him."

As Time Goes By played.

A dreamy piece that pushed her libido into overdrive. She sucked Farron's back and stroked the separation between his cheeks.

He squirmed. "In we go."

They dropped down. Water flew up. Her eye lights made the bubbles citrine-yellow, a beautiful and festive color. Like rubber balls, she and Farron bounced back and broke the surface, separated for the moment.

He pushed sodden hair from his face. "You all right?" Panic swept his features. "Can't you swim?"

Not with something tugging her ankles. She searched the pool, worried about a sea monster he might keep as a pet. The only thing beneath them was the Tropic of Pleasure logo. She slapped water, trying to keep from going under. "You're pulling me down."

"Me?" He alternated between a wounded look and smiling wickedly. "Guess I'll have to rescue you."

She suspected that wasn't going to happen. He wanted to play.

After a roguish wink, he dove in.

Ursula twisted away from his reach and kicked furiously. She broke his power hold at last and swam to the left.

He shot through the water faster than a torpedo, with her as his destination.

The theme song from *Jaws* played in her mind. She grabbed her knees, curled into a ball and sank. He zipped past. She swam in the opposite direction, her strokes strong and assured. Those lonely nights at the gym, when she'd done endless laps to burn off her sexual tension, were paying off.

Upon reaching the far end, she stopped. He wasn't around. There were no bubbles or waves from him, either. She lifted her face. He wasn't hovering above. Nor was he in the next room. A monstrous flat-screen TV dominated the area.

A splash broke out behind her.

She screeched.

With his arm around her waist, Farron swam them to the swallow end and rested his back against the smooth concrete. She feasted on his mouth. His lips were slightly chilled from water that didn't match his inner heat.

He cupped her ass and pulled her up. Once she had her legs wrapped around him, he entered.

Her head fell to his shoulder. His rod drained her of any power she'd assumed. In here, he ruled. She didn't mind. He'd always ask, never take, making certain they both got their due. Water made them essentially weightless and lovemaking super easy. They glided into and away from each other, their mouths always joined. His fierce kiss turned gentle and loving. Locked within each other's embrace, they fought climax but lost.

Okay, they won, too. Her giggling, him laughing.

He eased her hair behind her ear. She did the same with his and tightened her muscles around his shaft. Amazing. "Call me crazy, but you're still hard."

"Occupational hazard."

Or she'd done that to him. Preferring that scenario, Ursula batted her eyelashes. "Maybe I'm not working you hard enough."

She pulled away effortlessly and swam to the steps.

"Hey, come back here."

Holding on to the stair rails, she pulled herself from the water. "When you catch me."

He jumped out of the pool with more grace than a cat and looked down at her from the top step, his rigid rod pointed at her mouth. "I just did."

"Try again." She unfurled her wings and flew to the ceiling.

"Oh, please." He released his feathers, massive, powerful and pure black.

A demon among demons.

She flew through the penthouse. He followed in hot pursuit. They dipped, swayed and careened around corners, accompanied by Maroon 5's *Moves Like Jagger*. Farron sang along with Adam Levine, both their voices surprisingly good.

When Christina Aguilera came on, Ursula joined in and missed some notes.

Farron didn't laugh. He either hadn't noticed or didn't care that she was imperfect.

With their wings keeping them afloat, they boogied to the music. Her glowing eyes swept them and the surroundings like a strobe light. On the tune's last whistle and note, they collapsed into each other's arms, her wings wrapped around him, his around her.

They floated to the leather sofa in his video room, wings retracted, and cuddled. If this wasn't the best night ever, she didn't know what was. "Need to sleep?"

"No. You?"

"Uh-uh. Hungry?"

He slipped his hand between her thighs. "We just ate."

"Not food with calories, we didn't."

A banquet table materialized, piled with numerous chocolate desserts, a full ham, prime rib, roasted pork, chicken, countless sides and booze. "Love your service. But my thighs and hips aren't going to be as happy."

"Trying for another spanking?"

"The first was fabulous. I can't believe I existed so long without it."

"I can. This lifestyle isn't you."

An éclair flew their way. He caught the treat and handed it to her.

She wanted to bite him for ruining their good time and circling back to the same problem they could solve together, if he'd only believe in their relationship as she did. "Thanks. You're wrong. Everything we did tonight is me."

The TV flicked on. Not a program or porn but rather monitors in the club. Guest laughter and activities held his attention.

Ursula would have turned the stupid thing off but there wasn't a remote, switch or power cord around. Unable to stop the video feed, she regarded Farron and waited for him to acknowledge her.

Farron slouched on the sofa and stared at the TV screen without seeing it. Ursula's high beams shone on his face. Whenever she was excited or upset, her eyes glowed more brightly, giving away her emotions. No different from his pupil flames. The moment anything bummed him out, the fire shrank to pinpoints. He figured it was practically invisible now.

Tonight had been a colossal mistake, making him want her more, and it wasn't only the sex. Truthfully, that was the smallest part of what he craved about her. She was wicked fun, didn't care how she looked and could swim or fly with the best.

Ursula was like dating an easygoing guy with the bonus of her having boobs, a pussy and soft, smooth skin.

They weren't dating and had to end this here and now, like adults. He looked over, squinted and turned away.

"The light's bothering you. I can close my eyes or wear shades. Do you have any?"

He could make them appear, but didn't want to hurt her feelings. At least not more than he was going to. Frowning at the TV, he practiced his it's-me-not-you speech then leaned up and stared. "How in the hell?"

Empty booze bottles littered Stefin's, Anatol's and Taro's cages. Buck naked, they rocked, swinging the enclosures. They also sung loudly and laughed.

"Lilith!" Farron's voice boomed in here and from the screen.

She stopped pouring the vamp's drink. "What?"

That word again. He wanted to scream. "I told you not to give the prisoners any booze."

"I didn't. Blame the ladies."

The shot zoomed out showing female demons beneath the cages. They waved liquor at the guys. Stefin snatched more vodka and flexed his cock. The women went wild.

Farron switched off the image and frowned at Ursula. "See that? That's why you don't belong here."

"Because the guys are having fun? You put them in cages in a bar, I didn't."

"Drave did that. I never touched their sorry asses. You, on the other hand, had them bring you here. Can't you see you don't belong in my fucking world?"

"Why are you so angry?"

Because she'd been slipping away from him the moment they'd met. "I'm not."

"Your eyes say otherwise."

Hers had dimmed considerably, her mood oddly calm. The way women behaved when they knew they were right and had no doubt about winning against a guy.

He buried his head in his hands. "Even if you committed the grossest crime ever *and* bugged the shit out of everyone here by passing out pamphlets, you'd still be too good for this place. Face it, you'll never be a demon."

"I wasn't planning on becoming one. Is that what you'd like me to be?"

"Fuck no. Since we met, I've been trying to save you from yourself and keep failing miserably. Which only leaves one thing in order for us to work as a couple. I'd have to change." He rolled his eyes. "Like that's going to happen. If you think I'm going to turn into a good angel even with the service working on me round the clock, seven days a week for eternity, I have news for you. Ain't gonna happen."

"I don't want it to."

He leaned away. "You're talking crazy. Something has to give."

"No, it doesn't. The soul wants equality for all."

Exactly what he'd said to Becca without planning to. "Where'd you hear that?"

"Nowhere. It just came to me. But it's the truth. We're all okay as we are. No one should become a person they aren't deep inside, especially in the hope that someone else will want them. You're perfect. I wouldn't change a thing."

"I stink of sulfur."

"You smell of it and musk. Unbelievably hot."

"I own BDSM clubs."

"This place rocks."

"I live in fucking Hell!"

He removed the ocean scene as he'd done earlier. A volcano erupted, shooting a fireball that hit a flying monster squarely in its chest. On a horrific squeal, the thing caught fire and dropped to the ground. After its wings flapped a few times, it gave up the fight. Lava rolled over the remains.

New explosions and flames tinted Ursula's face deep red. She turned from the gruesome scene to him. "When the guys and I arrived here, it didn't look this bad out there. Are you tweaking it to scare me?"

He'd never confess. "It's still ugly."

"As compared to other places. However, I'm sure it has its charms."

"It's Hell, for Chrissake, and I live here."

"For now."

"What?" He couldn't believe this. "You're planning to smuggle me into Heaven?"

"Even if I could, you wouldn't be any happier there than I was."

"Was? You're moving? Uh-uh. You can't stay here."

"I wasn't planning to. We can visit, though."

"We? Now I'm not staying here, either?"

"Do you want to?"

Farron opened his mouth and closed it. He'd never considered the question. Being a fallen angel was written in stone. The job description never changed. "This is the only place I belong."

"You belong with me. We belong together." She searched his face, her irises a soft gold rather than blinding. "Tell me you don't want that and I'll leave. Say you don't love me and I'll never bother you again."

He should. He had to. "I can't."

She threw her arms around him. "I love you, too."

He'd never been as grateful or more afraid and held on to her like a drowning man. "I don't know what this means or where we could go together. No one in the universe will ever accept us as a couple."

"Then we'll have to change that and their minds. Anything's possible."

She was talking crazy hope again. Strangely enough, he wouldn't have wanted her any other way. "Where do we go from here?"

"Back to where we met."

"The service?"

"New Orleans. That's where we'll build our future."

Epilogue

Eight months later…

The October afternoon was wonderfully mild, high-seventies, the sky Wedgwood blue. Perfect for a celebration.

It wasn't every day a good angel got married, especially to a badass demon with killer dimples.

Ursula beamed at Farron, unafraid to be who she was, a woman hopelessly in love. He winked. A soft breeze ruffled his dark hair. The sun seemed to shine only on him.

Heather had suggested Couturie Forest for the nuptials, specifically a grassy clearing near water flanked by majestic live oaks, sweet gums and magnolias. Rich earth and vegetation perfumed the air. Daemon waved to his satyr friends hidden within the leaves and shadows. He used to live here with them when he'd had horns, hooves and a tail. Today, he looked unusually civilized dressed in a tuxedo. The same as Farron's other groomsmen—Stefin, Taro, Anatol, Rafael, Eric and Gabe.

Being a NOLA cop, Gabe had pulled strings to make certain this area remained private for the wedding party. MJ had also helped, granting wishes to keep the outside world at bay. She, Heather, Wynona, Becca and Zoe were Ursula's bridesmaids, beautiful in their rose pantsuits. Constance wore a pink-and-white striped gown. As a licensed minister for supernaturals, she'd officiated gladly.

No one downed Farron any longer. He was one of the gang. Family now.

With the vows over, the guys undid their bowties and ditched their jackets. The ladies kicked off their heels in favor of burying their toes in the velvety grass. Everyone laughed, talked and feasted on the banquet Becca had provided the human way, with a credit card, no magic. Despite her studies, her spells were still more miss than hit. Thankfully, her business skills were top-notch.

Ursula shared a hungry kiss with her new husband, leaving his lips bruised and pupils flaming. "Have I told you how beautiful you are?"

He laughed. "I'm supposed to say that to you." He rested his forehead against hers. "You are."

Her eyes weren't glowing any longer, except during their most intimate times, proving her arousal. Thankfully, his wings were as black as ever, a good color on him. She didn't want Farron changing. Nor did he expect that of her. Of course, she had dolled up for today's event. Her ivory dress boasted a sweetheart neckline embellished with fabric roses and a flouncy knee-length skirt.

What she planned to wear tonight and during the rest of their honeymoon wasn't as innocent. After Rome, they'd journey to France, Spain, England, Universal Studios Hollywood and Magic Mountain, then return here to the modest home they'd bought. There, they'd resume their work as supernatural political activists, educating those like them that the constant battle between good and evil wasn't necessary. Everyone needed to chill. As Farron had.

She worried more about his businesses than he did. "You're sure Drave knows how to run things while we're gone?"

Farron had promoted him from security chief to COO for the clubs.

"Taught him everything I know." He slipped a stuffed mushroom into her mouth.

She moaned at the decadent bacon and cheese flavors. "At least you're only a phone call away."

"Not me. Gigi's there to help him out."

Ursula fought laughter. "Poor girl. She tries."

In the past months, they'd become friends. Many demons had embraced Farron's odd choice in a woman and welcomed Ursula unreservedly. She'd done the same with them, though there was still a huge hurdle to surmount. "Thanks for inviting S today."

Farron had done so in person, no less, with her in tow. Satan claimed Farron had lost his mind to hook up with a good angel. Composed, he'd answered the only way he could. The soul demanded equality for all.

After making a show of gagging, Satan had threatened her with possession and Farron with expulsion from Hell. A first for a demon. Satan usually dumped the problem cases at From Crud to Stud. In any event, what he'd said was an empty threat. Farron was his cousin, blood if you will, at least figuratively. She was part of their inner circle, too. More than once, he'd brought her to his clubs for a night out. No one said a word against them nor did Satan get inside her head.

Farron shrugged. "Fat lot of good the invite did. He didn't come."

She cradled his cheek. "We'll have other parties. He'll attend them. Oliver will, too."

He'd been her heavenly supervisor and was a stickler for protocol. She'd given him two weeks' notice when she quit her admin job, explaining automation would eventually replace her, anyway, saving him and the operation a few bucks.

Oliver hadn't been amused, nor had he responded to her wedding invitation. Heaven was off-limits to her, the pearly gates on lockdown.

The only thing she regretted was everyone's stubbornness. "Someday, they'll be our friends again."

"Please don't hold your breath."

"Are you sorry about this or us?"

"Never." He cupped her face. "You're my world. I don't care what anyone else thinks about something that's so right. I can't live without you."

The best vow ever.

She hugged him. "I promise we'll change things."

They'd work on the beings down here first, convincing angels and demons there wasn't a need to fight. The feud between the Big Guy and S had gone on too long. Time for a truce. A universe without warfare. A place to understand and love.

It wouldn't be easy, but with Farron beside her, they wouldn't fail. She squeezed harder.

A smartphone played Santana's *Evil Ways*, the tune filling the balmy air. Zoe's sigh was as rough as her voice. She reached inside her purse. "I'll bet something's happened at the service."

"It'll have to wait." Becca pointed her fork. "This is Ursula and Farron's day. Whatever's going on at the office, we'll deal with it later. Turn off the phone."

Zoe did. Everyone else easily resumed their conversations, meals and laughter.

Farron kissed Ursula's fingers. Holding hands, they fed each other, refusing to allow anything to interfere with their stunning happiness that was more than right.

It was epic and the start of something big.

Want to see more like this?
Here's a taster for you to enjoy!

Vegas Mythbehaving:
Miss Predictable
Kelly Ethan

Excerpt

"Oh, damn." Cassandra flinched as a jagged blue bolt of lightning sizzled overhead. She planted her foot on the accelerator and roared up the curved driveway of the Olympus Hotel and Casino, praying she didn't hit one of the many peacocks that wandered throughout the enclosed landscape.

Reaching the entrance foyer, she ground to a halt with a screech of brakes and, releasing the seatbelt, threw herself out of the vehicle. At least that was the idea. In reality her foot caught in the belt and she ended up on hands and knees on the cobbled courtyard. She scrambled to her feet and backed away from the car... Just in time.

A new lightning spear hit the roof of the vehicle. The hood flew open with a monstrous belch. Black smoke billowed high into the sky. A bellhop scampered past and screeched to an undignified stop next to the dying Chrysler, his mouth open as he stared at the charred mess.

Cassandra ignored him. Instead, she bared her teeth at the dark cloud hovering above what was left of her car and flashed a one-fingered salute at the gods. "Bloody hell. What next?" She raised her voice. "Any other natural disasters you want to throw at me?"

On the day her mother disappears, suddenly ferocious heat-seeking lighting stalks her? What storm follows a person at all, let alone from Chicago to Las Vegas?

Speak of the evil black in the sky… Cassandra cringed as another charge of lightning-fed electricity traced a path across the driveway then circled back behind the peacocks that clustered in a group in the shade of a nearby bush. The birds, already upset by the noise of the thunder, set up a frantic cry. Another follow-up flash was enough to send them in a last-ditch charge.

As one, the feathered flock raced across the driveway toward the apparent safety of the foyer. On the heels of another roll of thunder, the peacocks increased their pace until they bobbled like frantic aerobics instructors on steroids. As they reached the cobbled area in front of the open door, Cassandra found herself surrounded. She flung her arms out, trying to dodge the peacocks with little steps in an effort to get out of their way. A sharp beak prodded at her bottom and, with a shriek, she rubbed her offended posterior. Well, so much for that.

The birds surged into the building. Bellowed curses followed their entrance. Cassandra, along with the bellhop, moved closer to the door then peered inside. She couldn't help but wince at the agitated peacocks attacking the many marble statues scattered throughout the lobby.

She hugged herself tightly around her middle and backed away. She grimaced and shook her head. *Another apology.* The list grew longer every minute. The car, the feathered freaks. But weren't hotel employees trained for different kinds of situations? She wondered if killer storms were part of their training package.

"Problems?"

Another question. Why did everyone ask questions?

"Everything's fine. It's just Beat On Cassandra Week." Not a horrible answer. Twist her words a tad and no one got hurt.

Her run of bad luck had started seven days ago when her apartment had died as a result of storm damage. A deluge of water had descended on the apartment roof and flooded her place, making the building uninhabitable. No wonder the insurance company cursed the Troy name. She'd had no choice but to camp with her mom.

Cassandra curled her lip at her well-meaning-mother-avoidance plan. *No paranormal interaction needed, just bury myself in work.* Except three hours after she'd shifted into her mother's one-bedroom apartment above the shop where she ran her business, Cassandra had found herself without a job. Wouldn't you know it? The library where she'd worked had closed owing to a mold and mildew problem.

Then what does Mom do? She runs off for a weekend away and here I am a week later—no parent in sight. Cassandra snorted. What was worse was that *she* was supposed to look after the business.

Her mother ran a little shop selling all kinds of occult paraphernalia. Old books, crystals, wands and a myriad other things people in the woo-woo trade seemed to think was necessary. Total bunkum, as far as Cassandra was concerned.

The main focus of the business, though, was her mother's tarot readings and crystal ball gazing. And she'd been left to run it? Damn difficult when she didn't believe in any of this bull. The shop she could have dealt with, but the rest? No way, no how! It felt too much like suckering people in and taking their money under false pretenses. In fact, the whole thing grated on Cassandra's last nerve. It was time to drag her runaway mom back home and restore reality to its rightful place.

Focus, Cassandra. She dragged herself back to the present and shot a perfunctory smile at the person standing behind her. Okaaay, not the bellhop as she'd assumed! Whoa, romance hero central. *Heathcliff, your doppelganger's alive and well in Vegas.* Black hair and dark eyes gave him an aura of broody sex appeal, but there was something about him…

"Beat on this loveliness? Surely sacrilege?" He licked his lips.

Shudder. "The gods alone know what planned hell is next," she responded.

Question after question. The week from hell after her mother had disappeared followed by a mad flight to Vegas. That was bad enough, but now she'd been cursed with out-of-control honesty. Friends, sleazy neighbors, everyone got the truth treatment. But if she didn't speak, razors gripped her throat. Oh, it was definitely time to get answers. Woo-woo weird equaled her mother, not her. And an inability to lie was not only beyond strange, it was inconvenient to boot.

Cassandra winced as the guy let his gaze drift over her rumpled shirt, creased pants and wild hair. She looked like an escapee from a fashion asylum. She glared at her smoky car again. *The gods suck.*

"Those that rule on high are duplicitous by nature," he said in answer to her earlier comment about the gods. "By the way, I'm Assie. Are you going to be staying with us here at the hotel?"

At her nod, he moved closer. "In that case, if you need me…for anything, call the desk. They always know where I am." He ran his palm along her arm to her hand and pressed a light kiss to the back of it before he prowled away.

The hair lifted on the back of Cassandra's neck. Good-looking guy, but he made her feel as if a whole army of boot-scooting ants had danced up her spine. Weird. With a fatalistic shrug, she turned her back on the driveway debacle and marched into the hotel. Once at the reception desk, she placed her bag on the counter and waited. And waited... Until she lost patience and coughed loud and long. The receptionist jumped, but pasted on a fake 'How can I help you?' smile.

"I need your cheapest room and what number is Cassandra Troy Senior in, please?" *And don't ask me any hard questions.*

The young woman behind the desk crossed her arms. "I'm sorry, miss, but we have a reunion here at the moment. The hotel's full. You could try the Bellagio next door."

Warmth rushed over Cassandra's face. *Temper. Control the temper. Save it for your mother.* She repeated the mantra. Her craptastic day wasn't the receptionist's fault — it was her mom's. Cassandra moderated her tone and spoke in a quiet voice. "I don't care if there's a Perverts R Us convention here. Please, help me find my mother and get me a room."

Cassandra's fingertips tingled with a burst of electricity and the temptation to point at the poor woman rode high. With her luck and all the weird things that had happened to her this past week, the receptionist would keel over, and she'd end up in jail for grievous bodily harm or something.

The young blonde hotel employee glanced at her computer. "I'll see what I can do."

"Please. And I need to find my mother. She's a guest here." *At least I hope she is.* Cassandra sagged against the desk and concentrated on her biggest problem of all — her mom.

"I'm sorry, we can't divulge information about our guests without prior approval."

At the return of the receptionist's snooty tone, Cassandra's palms stung suddenly. She stared down at them. She hadn't even realized she'd clenched her hands into fists. Yet here she was drawing blood.

She flexed her fingers and let the woman have it. "Listen, chicky, Mom has disappeared. The night before she left, she dumped her shop on me — because, of course, I'm reliable and predictable." She imitated her mother. *"Leave it to Miss Predictable to run The Oracle."*

"Ah, isn't The Oracle a Greek lady who tells the future?" The receptionist stepped back out of spitting range, her eyes wide.

An easy question as long as Cassandra didn't lose her temper. "She's a distant relative." She counted to five before leveling her gaze on the girl. "Please, before I lose my sanity, *I need to find my mother.*"

"Can I help?"

A delicious, warm heaviness pooled in the base of her stomach at the husky velvet tones. Cassandra rubbed at her chest. A dull thud double-pumped in her ribcage. Her nipples peaked under her blouse until the pebbled tips ached. His voice alone made her want to dry-hump him right here in the hotel lobby. Compelled, she spun toward the owner of the sultry tones.

Oh my God. Pay dirt. Must be a hunky Men R Us convention. First the guy outside, now this man. Cassandra faked a cough and wiped her chin in case of drool. Man, she hoped her loose words didn't stab her in her ego.

"I need a room and I'm too angry and arrogant to take no for an answer." *And if asked a question, I can't lie. Oh, and I live to humiliate myself.*

She prayed her compulsive words didn't insult the delicious man next to her. And a dish he was. The outside far exceeded the voice. In fact, he resembled a Greek god. Thick black hair curled around a perfect face. His olive complexion tied in with her hot deity image and black eyes gleamed at her from his six foot height. *Wow. I'd have to stand on a box to kiss this guy or risk neck cramps.*

"Miss, can you hear me? Do you need to sit? Or a glass of water?"

Off balance, Cassandra wobbled. She leaned against the desk for support.

"I need a room and Cassandra Troy."

Sign up for our newsletter and find out about all our romance book releases, eBook sales and promotions, sneak peeks and FREE romance books!

About the Author

Tina is an Amazon and international bestselling novelist in erotic, paranormal, contemporary and historical romance for traditional publishers and indie. Booklist, Publisher's Weekly, Romantic Times and numerous online sites have praised her work. She's won Readers' Choice Awards, was named a finalist in the EPIC competition, received a Book of the Year award, The Golden Nib Award, awards of merit in the RWA Holt Medallion competitions, and second place in the NEC RWA contests. She's featured in the Novel & Short Story Writer's Market. Before penning romances, she worked at a major Hollywood production company in Story Direction.

Tina loves to hear from readers. You can find her contact information, website details and author profile page at http://www.totallybound.com